ARTIFICIAL ATTRACTION

Brandie Van Hartesvelt, winner of a writing guild's Best Upcoming Young Author award, spins a tantalizing tale of secret identity, forbidden love, and a choice poised to doom the world.

When talented coder Amara Ashford lands her dream job at Hyperionix, she's isolated on a top-secret project with her boss, brilliant scientist and ethical AI activist Ethan Trask. The pair is tasked with harnessing Kryplex, the only energy source capable of shattering the Zeraphin Limit and powering teleportation, while Amara, still reeling from a broken engagement, must resist her new lab partner's charm.

But Kryplex is a volatile substance, and trial runs are going alarmingly awry. As corporate pressure mounts to unveil the new technology, Amara uncovers a centuries-old secret in the company's code—and a devastating link to Ethan.

Torn between duty and desire, Amara must decide whether to expose Ethan's identity... or surrender to a love that could cost humankind its future.

A TANTALIZING TALE OF
SECRET IDENTITY, FORBIDDEN
LOVE, AND A CHOICE POISED
TO DOOM THE WORLD

ARTIFICIAL ATTRACTION

a sci-fi sweet

romance

BRANDIE VAN HARTESVELT

ARTIFICIAL ATTRACTION

A SCI FI SWEET ROMANCE

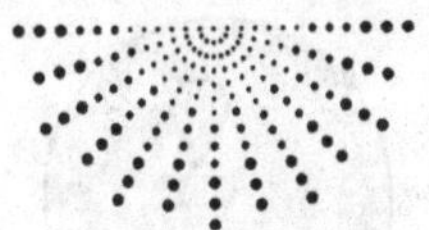

BRANDIE VAN HARTESVELT

Copyright © 2026 The Narrative Path, LLC
House Springs, Missouri, USA

ISBN-13: 979-8-9985748-3-2
Paperback First Edition
10 9 8 7 6 5 4 3

To my friends at AutoCrit—thanks for helping shape my author voice

CHAPTER ONE

$\mathcal{A}$mara stood outside the conference room door, eyes closed as she focused on calming her first-day nerves. She wiped her palms on her pants, tucked her short brown curls behind her ear, and walked in.

The air shimmered to life, and the silhouette of a man in a suit appeared.

"Good morning, Amara. Welcome," said the man, flashing a smile that revealed straight, sparkling teeth. "I'm Ethan."

Amara's mouth dropped. "No way! You… you're Ethan Trask! I *just* saw you speak on the panel for the Global Committee for the Safe and Ethical Use of Artificial Intelligence."

"Um, yes, that was me," he said, shifting his tie.

"I looked you up after. Your list of patents is quite impressive," she said demurely.

"I… um… well, yes, thank you," he sniffed.

"And you're here with me… well, virtually, anyway," she said, lacing her fingers under her chin and beaming a smile.

Ethan blinked, then shook his head. "I'm responsible for

leading all orientation sessions here at Hyperionix Technology. It allows me to meet the company's finest new talent."

Did that gorgeous, insanely talented man just call *her* talented?

"Nice to meet you," she said, a hint of color rising to her freckled cheeks.

His piercing blue eyes penetrated the space between them, and, for the briefest moment, she swore he could peer clear into her soul. She shook the silly notion from her head —he was obviously just looking at the camera. She needed to pull herself together, stat!

"Please, have a seat and make yourself comfortable. It's just you and me today. Before you ask: no, I don't usually participate in one-on-one orientation sessions. But the work you published on the CLEO project caught my attention. Your findings were groundbreaking—and personally, I don't think the implications are fully realized as of yet, or any of the benefits, either," he said.

She blinked in stunned silence as she fought against the flush creeping across her face. How could such an accomplished and confident man admire *her* achievements? Sliding into her seat, when she finally mustered the courage to turn her head towards the screen, Amara found herself face-to-face with Ethan. She studied the clean, handsome angles of his chin and the way his lusciously thick, jet-black hair was so precisely cut to flatter his bone structure.

"Stop it!" Amara smacked her forehead.

"Um... Amara, is something wrong?" he asked.

Wincing, she racked her brain for an excuse. *Any* excuse. Seriously... anything was better than confessing the thoughts she was trying to purge from her mind.

"Yeah, sorry, I... something buzzed my ear," she said sheepishly.

Ethan nodded. "I see," he said evenly. "Are you ready to learn about what you've been brought here to work on?"

Her stomach balled itself up into a knot. She'd just been ready, eager even! But that was before she knew one of the world's most brilliant minds would be doing the schooling.

"I guess," she said with a gulp.

"Imagine this," Ethan said, sweeping his hands in a half circle. "No commute time. Zero emissions. Instantaneous travel from point A to point B."

"You mean teleportation?" Amara asked, fighting to subdue the frightened edge to her voice, lest she reveal she was in *way* over her head.

"Indeed," he said, the twinkle in his eye making her shift uncomfortably.

Her mind was slow, but it still functioned. Teleportation wasn't possible—that'd been proven! Well, not precisely proven, but there was some reason it wasn't possible. If only she could remember what that was. Not a law, but something else, maybe. A ceiling? No. A limit? Yes, that's it!

"Now wait a second! What about the Zeraphin Limit? Has it been discredited?" she asked.

"Not at all! It's as valid as the day Sir Edward Zeraphin published his groundbreaking research," Ethan said, his tone insinuating he was holding something back.

She bit her lip. "Well, if the limit is still valid, then…"

Amara's gaze flitted to her upper left as she worked out the details. There was a missing connection—she just needed to figure it out. It'd help if she could remember the law.

"Okay," she said, intaking a large breath and slowly blowing it out. "The Zeraphin Limit says teleportation *is* possible, but the problem is… if I remember correctly… that it goes beyond humanity's capabilities to power it?"

"Excellent!" Ethan said with a clap of his hands.

Her eyebrows skyrocketed. "So are you saying we have

access to a substance capable of flipping Zeraphin's equation into the positive? That's... that's insane!"

"Shhhh," cautioned Ethan, his eyes widening. "The answer to your question is yes. It's something called Kryplex, but we'll learn more about that later—*after* you sign those clearance documents to your left. Then we can only speak about it within designated secure zones. Our work lab is one of those, but this orientation room, unfortunately, is not."

"*Our* work lab?" she asked, her ankles rubbing together.

"Indeed! The project you'll be working on is classified. Only a few individuals know of its existence. I'll be your primary collaborator," he chuckled. "Heck, I'll be your *only* collaborator for the foreseeable future."

Amara gulped. "I'll be working with... um... you?"

Ethan flashed a dazzling smile. "Yep! It'll just be you and me, so I hope you'll be comfortable with us spending a *lot* of time together."

Amara's eyes closed as heat flushed up her navel.

"I think I could get used to that," she said, her head swimming.

She just didn't know if she *should*.

CHAPTER TWO

$\mathcal{A}$mara stumbled out of the conference room in a daze. She was going to help make teleportation a reality! She *should* be elated—or at the very least, terrified. But she couldn't stop thinking about how soft and kissable her new coworker's lips looked, and wondering if they would feel as velvety smooth as his voice. The encounter had been intense... the way she was so sure he *knew* her. It was only light particles over an airescreen, yet she swore he was right next to her. How was it possible to feel such palpable tension through a virtual screen?

She sent a message to ask her best friend for advice. Minutes later, as she closed the doors of her new campus suite behind her, she opened an airescreen.

"Who is he?! Spill!" Mel demanded, hands on her hips.

"Hello to you, too, Mel. I enjoyed my orientation. Thanks for asking."

"I'm sure you did!" she said cheekily. "Now, who's the hunk you texted me about?!"

"There's no *hunk*. It's just a coworker who's hot... *really* freaking hot. But that's not even the best part! He's absolutely

5

brilliant, Mel. I could paper my desk with the list of patents this man has."

Mel smiled. "Sounds right up your alley."

"Ugh! But you should see his eyes, Mel, I could melt in them," Amara said breathily.

Mel giggled.

"I'm going to have a heckuva time staying focused here, you know. My new project sounds *ah-mazing*! But it hasn't even begun to sink in yet… not really. Ethan is all I can think about since I've met him!" she huffed.

Mel snorted. "Which was what, thirty seconds ago?!"

"Two or three minutes," Amara answered coyly.

Her friend shook her head. "Gimme the deets on that new gig of yours."

Amara kicked at the ground. "I can't—it's confidential. It's theoretical science, but that's all I can tell you."

"Oh, don't give me that! You've gotta be able to tell me something," Mel said.

Amara shrugged. "Sorry, I signed a legal doc."

Mel stared at the camera, lips pursed. "Surely that doesn't apply to me, your bestest friend in the entire world?"

Amara's lips curled. "I'll be working on something that's going to change humanity. Something that everyone thought was impossible, something even *I* thought was impossible… until today."

"And you're sure you can't give me a teensy little hint?" Mel asked.

"I'm serious, Mel! I don't know if I can pull this off," Amara said, her breath coming in short spurts. "I've dreamt of working for Hyperionix since I was a little girl. But what I'm being asked to do has never been attempted before, and I'm kinda terrified I'm gonna screw it all up."

"Hey, hey—it's going to be okay! You're the most brilliant

person I know, and if anyone can make the impossible happen, it's you," soothed Mel.

"I wish I had that much faith in myself, because now I have to partner with the most brilliant person I know, and even *he's* stumped."

"I wanna hear about the future Mr. Ashford. What's his name?" Mel asked with a shoulder shimmy.

"Ethan, and let's not rush to the altar just yet, k?" said Amara, hoping Mel couldn't see the heat that rose to her cheeks.

"Hmmm… could be sexier, but it works," Mel said flippantly.

Amara rolled her eyes. "Like he could choose his name, Mel."

"Yeah, yeah, yeah. How old is he?" Mel asked.

Amara bit her lip. There'd been a few lines that lingered after he smiled, but there'd certainly been no grey in his locks.

"Early thirties, maybe? A little bit older than me, but not much," answered Amara.

"Young enough to date, that's what's important," said Mel.

"Whoa! Slow down. There are… like… I dunno, a *million* things wrong with that."

"Like?"

Amara scoffed. "Like he's a coworker, and like I've just started this job! And like I care about my career a *heckuva* lot more than I care about some guy!"

"That's what makes this perfect, miss chronically-over-worked-and-single. You'll be working with this one—you won't need to choose."

"Yeah, but if things blow up, I could lose my job," said Amara.

"Is he your boss?" Mel asked.

"I don't know *who* he is, but he has high clearance and knows a lot about the company," she answered.

"Well, you're exceptionally brilliant and could work anywhere. But love isn't so easy to find, May."

Her friend's special nickname for her, the one that only ever crossed Mel's lips, reeled her in.

Amara flopped back against her seat. "I'm not sure I believe in love, Mel."

"Whoa, hold up! How can you say love's not for you?! You've already found it once, you're gonna find it again."

An empty ache flashed across Amara's heart. "Come on, Mel. The universe already turned me down."

"Oh, no no no... May... don't say that. Just because Jeremy—"

"Don't you say his name!" Amara warned, her eyebrows sternly raised and finger pointed at the camera.

Mel cocked her face to the side and swallowed. "Fine. But just because what's-his-face got cold feet a month before your guys' wedding does *not* mean the universe has sealed your fate! Besides, the guy was all wrong for you, May."

"Hmph. Tell me how you *really* feel there, Mel," said Amara.

"It's been three years! I've waited *three whole years* to sour his name. You were never yourself around him, or you weren't the May I knew, anyway. You just seemed... well... dimmed."

Amara steepled her fingers. "I felt like myself... I think? I mean, I loved him. We planned to spend the rest of our lives together."

Mel threw up her palms. "You two have *nothing* in common. You're a brilliant scientist, and he has the IQ of a freaking potato!"

"But he was gorgeous, and he wanted *me*," sighed Amara, her eyes going distant. "I don't know what it was when I was with him, but I always felt *ah-mazing*. Like no one else in the world existed except for me."

"Yet you were always trying to earn his attention a *teensy* bit more than he was trying to earn yours," said Mel, gazing sternly at the camera between her pinched thumb and index finger.

"That's not true," pouted Amara.

"And I *still* think it's mighty suspicious how quickly he and Veronica paired up after you two split. I think all that one-and-only crap is just that—crap! He was playing you from the get-go. You want my honest opinion?" asked Mel, pointing her chin at the camera. "I think he was more into you for your looks than anything else. You always seemed like... I don't know... like you were an accessory on his arm."

Amara shuddered, remembering how Jeremy would get upset at any slight imperfection in her appearance. An imperfection in her was an imperfection in him, he'd say when something wasn't up to snuff. It left her on edge and worrying about every little thing, from an extra ounce on the scale to peeling skin from an unanticipated sunburn.

"How did I fall for someone like that, Mel? Why didn't I see through it? Or see it coming, or something?" Amara asked, resting her cheek on her fist.

"Come on, May! You're not being fair to yourself. There's a reason they say love is blind—people constantly get duped."

"I don't know, Mel... there's gotta be something I missed. If I don't find it, how can I keep it from happening again?" asked Amara, her lip trembling as her brave resolve began to crumble.

"You can't. There's no guarantee it won't happen again, or that you won't get your heart broken. You deserve someone a bajillion times better than potato-face. Someone who wants all of you."

"Potato-face," Amara broke out laughing. "I love it! That's gonna be his name now!"

"Great! Now put 'ole potato-face behind you and find someone better," said Mel.

Amara's good cheer plummeted as her nails bit into her palm, carving half-moon divots. Someone better? According to Jeremy, she'd never find anyone better than him. And he'd been right, hadn't he?! Three years, and not a single person had ventured near. It was clear—love wasn't in the cards for her. She'd had her shot and struck out.

"I'm telling you, the universe has shut me down," Amara said, her jaw tightening.

"That's *so* not true, May. But—and you gotta pay attention here—you'll never find it if you don't try. So get to dating! Starting with that sizzling new coworker of yours," Mel said with a wink.

"Ugh. I can't find love with Ethan. Seriously, Mel, I just started this job, and I'm super excited about the work—more than I am about a guy, even if he *is* incredibly steamy. And sorta famous... at least in a nerdy kinda way."

"Do what you've gotta, May. But I'll be here to listen and cheer you on if you ever feel like looking past that," Mel said.

"Heh. No chance of that, but I'll humor you and say I'll try," she promised.

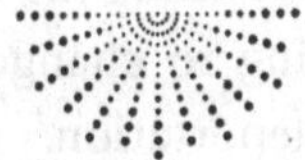

CHAPTER THREE

"Welcome, Amara," Ethan's hologram greeted her as she entered the lab.

The door shut automatically with a whoosh, the wind brushing the tails of her lab coat. Linoleum flooring gleamed as she turned circles, mouth agape. Workstation-topped desks occupied the room's center, while a kitchenette and table filled the far left corner. The back wall was composed entirely of floor-to-ceiling cabinets, and the right held workstations and consoles spanning its entire length. And, in the center of the wondrous room, was a floor-to-ceiling airescreen displaying a spluttering substance.

Amara's feet ambled towards the screen, her gaze transfixed. It was so blindingly white it should've left holes in her vision, yet somehow she managed to stare at it comfortably.

"What *is* that?" she asked, slowly circling the display.

"It's the future—a hyperdense element we've named Kryplex. It's a non-depleting energy source that outperforms nuclear-based options by a factor of at least five," explained Ethan.

"That's incredible," she said, studying the current as it traversed up one side and down the other.

"Our researchers discovered it at the bottom of the Veydran Sea, and a mere 15 liters is enough to power teleportation," he said.

Amara's head snapped up. "That hardly seems possible."

Ethan held his palm towards the screen. "Yet here it is—the substance that's going to change the face of humanity forever. Starting with teleportation."

Her mind spun. There had to be some other explanation, because with that much power, the Zeraphin limit would be bypassed instantly. And that would make teleportation possible, limited only by how quickly humans could finagle the logistics to harness it. And *that* would mean she would actually be part of this phenomenal, once-in-a-lifetime, scientific breakthrough.

The thought set her stomach ablaze with pain.

"The beta software for operating the prototype is nearly complete," Ethan said.

"Have you tested it?" she asked, cradling her stomach with her arm and trying not to grimace.

"Yes, but not on humans. There are a few issues to resolve—some behaviors we can't seem to isolate or control. That's why we hired you."

Amara's eyes widened as she backed away. "No, this has to be a mistake. I'm not qualified. I've never worked on anything even *remotely* like this."

"Have faith in yourself, Amara! *No one's* ever worked on anything like this before. Your work on CLEO was just as groundbreaking."

"Thank you," said Amara, glancing down and tucking her loose curls behind her ear.

Score one for today's first blush, which deepened further as a sudden desire to know what he smelled like overtook her... it'd be something alluring, no doubt. Her ankles rubbed together as she willed her mind to return to its professional setting. Reluctantly withdrawing her attention from the strange white substance and her uncannily handsome co-worker, she took in the splendor of the surrounding area.

Brushing her fingers across a desk, she sampled its luminescent, reflective surface. Cool and slick to the touch, the substance was alien to her, yet felt like stainless steel, only it maintained an inner warmth, almost a lively feel. All the equipment, desks, and even the cabinets were constructed of it.

"It's called shedonite. Wherever our teams find Kryplex, there's an abundance of this stuff lining the trenches. It's a crystalline stone that seems to replenish as quickly as we mine it," Ethan said.

She leaned in closer, unsure if the color was pearl or light pink, as it shifted with each turn of the head. "It's gorgeous... almost like opal in solid form."

"Heh. It's also a *lot* stronger than opal—twice as strong as steel, believe it or not—but it only weighs a third," he said.

Her eyes bulged. "That's *ah-mazing!* And wow... is it... is it *glowing?*"

He grinned, exposing his pearly white teeth. "Indeed, it is. We believe it contains particles that become charged by Kryplex, and those particles are luminescent, but we haven't been able to confirm that theory yet."

"So what, it just glows *forever?* It never stops?" she asked.

He shrugged. "We haven't been using it long enough to determine its lifespan."

"I can't decide if it feels warm," she said, brushing her fingers along various surfaces. "Is it heated?"

"It maintains the ambient temperature of the surrounding environment."

"So it's—"

"Never too hot, never too cold, and always within two degrees, no matter how rapidly the temperature swings," he answered.

Her mouth dropped. "Wow, you could have self-warming storage containers! Or even heated homes!"

"That's precisely the kind of ingenuity you were hired for!" Ethan said.

"What? No! Anyone would've drawn the same conclusion. Well, almost anyone," she said.

"Nonsense! I'm an expert at examining human behavior, and you are *far* above the average," he said, his piercing blue gaze narrowing intensely, causing her to fidget and turn away.

"Thanks," she said, scrunching her nose. "Smells almost like antiseptic, though."

Ethan steepled his fingers. "Yes, that's a pitfall we've not yet managed to overcome. It can't... well, it's never bothered me, but it does limit potential commercial uses of the stone. Your nose is detecting a harmless, off-putting gas produced by the crystalline stone's exposure to oxygen, likely linked to the chemical reaction that makes it glow."

"Sounds like shedonite is some pretty awesome stuff," Amara said as she trailed a glowing grain from one side of the wall to the other.

"It's also an insulator," he said.

Her eyebrows crinkled. "Huh? I'm not following."

"It doesn't allow electricity to flow through it, so it's similar to rubber, wood, plastic, or glass—all of which provide insulation."

"Okay..." Amara said, her chin pulled into a frown.

"It's also a highly effective thermal insulator. Its natural properties are ideal for portal construction, and it's been performing exceptionally well for that purpose. Now we've begun key test area integrations, including in our newest lab, which you're standing in," Ethan said, motioning widely with his arms.

"It's stunning! But what is it?" she asked.

"It's our future," Ethan said proudly.

She blinked. *Our* future?

"Welcome to the teleportation center command hub, or TECH for short," Ethan announced.

He'd interrupted Amara's thoughts, the stupid ones, the ones that took 'our future' to mean anything other than what it was—purely professional.

She needed to rein herself in. Pronto.

"*That's* what all this is?" she asked, gesturing at the dizzying array of equipment paneling the right side of the room.

"Yes, indeed! Not only is it convenient, but anchoring the TECH in our lab allows for zero-latency servers," he explained.

"I suppose that makes sense for testing," she said as she leisurely strolled the wall's length, her eyes drawn in all directions.

"If there's an issue during the middle of a trial, this becomes headquarters. Nice during work hours, but, unfortunately for us, trials are usually run off-hours," he said.

Amara shuddered involuntarily at the thought of being responsible for the fate of another human. She hadn't signed up for such a scary endeavor... not on purpose, anyway. It was excitement she wanted, not a potential lifetime's worth of trauma.

"Who runs the trials?" Amara asked.

"There's a team stationed in a facility up in the Arctic Circle, near our primary Kryplex mining site. A dedicated Kryplex core powers the portal."

Amara turned to look at the spot behind her shoulder

that Ethan indicated. A single red bulb, enclosed in a plastic cage, was mounted near the ceiling.

"That light turns solid red anytime the portal is in use," he explained. "It starts flashing if there's a problem."

Amara tilted her head. "Speaking of, you said there haven't been any human trials yet because of problems. What kind of problems?"

"The problems come when there's an issue mid-jump. Our initial test items disappeared and are *still* missing. Now everything returns, but not always in its entirety. Parts go missing, or get switched around."

"Eeek! Not something you want happening to a human," she said, scrunching her nose.

"Precisely the issue, but it won't be for much longer now that you're here. I'm confident of that," he said, his smile wide.

Amara gulped. *She* wasn't confident of her abilities to fix an unfixable problem—how could Ethan be so sure? How did he know *she*, of all people, would be able to fix what he couldn't?

And what if she failed?

"I dunno, Ethan," she said, shaking her head. "This scares me, like, hardcore. What if something goes wrong? Worse, what if it's *my* fault?"

"Nothing will be your fault, Amara. You didn't formulate the theory or build the infrastructure. All I'm asking you to do is improve an existing system. That's it," he said.

"Still, if something I did, if my code—"

"If *our* code fails, then it'll be a failure attributed to both of us," said Ethan. "I have to sign off on everything you do."

"It'd still be *my* mistake," she said.

"Nonsense! I'm fully responsible for anything I put my name to, and I do *not* do so lightly," he said, narrowing his gaze.

"Besides, anyone who gets into that portal is a volunteer. They'll sign a waiver, then go through a virtual attestation for each trip. We've already got several people willing to take the risk as soon as they see successful primate trials."

She winced. "Ugh! Animals too?!"

"No animals until inanimate objects are reliably making it through their jumps intact," he answered.

"Intact?!" she asked, a sick feeling sweeping her gut. She extended her trembling hand in front of the camera. "I don't know if I can do this. Look at me!"

Ethan frowned. "Aww, Amara, I love how deeply you care for others. And I understand how scared you must be, because I'm burdened with that same sense of responsibility for humanity. It's one of the reasons I chose *you* for this position. If you could only see yourself through my eyes, you'd never doubt yourself again."

Her knees buckled as a nauseating wave swept over her. Her gut warned that Ethan's confidence in her was misplaced, that she should run from Hyperionix immediately. She flickered between hot flashes as his trusting gaze flashed across her mind and freezing chills while she contemplated terminating her employment contract.

If only Hyperionix didn't employ two-thirds of the vracking planet.

CHAPTER FOUR

"$\mathcal{H}$onestly, Mel, if I couldn't have these airecalls with you, I think I'd go insane," Amara complained.

Mel giggled, her spunky black glasses bouncing up and down. "Surely there's someone more qualified than me to call for help, especially considering I don't even know how to code."

"That's precisely the problem! This project is *so* freaking top secret that I'm *literally* the only person who's physically in this lab. I'd love to call some of my old colleagues on the CLEO project, but clearance forbids it. Literally the *only* reason I can talk to you is because you're so freaking clueless about all this that no one would ever be able to make a case for espionage!" Amara said, tossing her hands up.

The girls broke out in laughter.

"You still shouldn't be talking to her in the lab," chided Ethan, his upper body popping up next to Amara's and causing her to startle.

"Ugh, I hate when you do that!" Amara complained.

One of Kryplex's breakthrough technologies was the

ability to spur an airescreen almost anywhere, as long as you had a special receiver. Only three of those currently existed in the world, and that lab contained one of them.

"Are you going to tattle on us?" Mel asked, resting her chin on her hands with a pout. "Quick, May! Flirt, would ya?!"

Amara blushed furiously, and it was several moments before she regained her composure enough to glare at her best friend properly.

"Gotta go, bye May," Mel chimed in a sing-song voice.

Amara's eyes widened. "Oh, don't you da—"

Mel winked as the screen disappeared.

"Ugh, what a freaking brat!" Amara kicked a cabinet near her feet.

"Hey now, that's certified Hyperionix technology you're assaulting over there. Wouldn't want to dock your paycheck," Ethan said, the glint in his eyes betraying his teasing.

She smiled, her frustrations forgotten in the mischievous twinkle of his gaze.

"I have an idea," she said with a clap of her hands. "How 'bout we work outside, get ourselves away from all this expensive equipment?"

"Sure," he said, flashing his pearly whites. "Let's do it."

A series of three chimes interrupted, and Amara's head snapped towards the ceiling.

"It's the intercom—an incoming announcement," Ethan explained.

The room dimmed as the blindingly white Kryplex was replaced by the full-sized hologram of a man who was waving enthusiastically. He donned a thick head of dark grey hair and a beard that reached his mid-chest.

"Goooood afternoon, valued Hyperionix employees, where we think of each other as family! I'm your chairman, Bill, and I'd like to invite *you* to a formal company dinner on *your* campus! That's right! Myself and the rest of the corporate team will come bearing some *really big* news! And no, it's not just dessert! So get ready, and mark your calendars for three months from today. I'll see you then!" he said with a wink as the screen disappeared.

She turned to Ethan. "Did you catch that?"

"Yeah, but it doesn't surprise me much. I'd already gotten wind of something like that, plus an order to clear my calendar for that very date," he answered, chin in hand.

"That doesn't sound like a coincidence to me," Amara said.

"No, it doesn't," Ethan answered. "Though I might wind up transferred before then. I've been told there's a request to have me moved to your campus, since we *are* the only two employees working this side of the project," Ethan said, brushing an ink-black wave of hair away from his blue eyes.

Her heart fluttered, but she pushed back at it, shoving it away and locking up all such desires. Besides, she'd just confirmed what she already knew—whoever Ethan was, he was important enough that corporate had called *him* personally. In other words, he was *way* above her on the totem pole —right up there in dating-your-boss territory. Amara congratulated herself on following her instincts and making the responsible choice. Love is temporary, but careers—those are forever, and they don't leave you hanging at the altar.

* * *

TEN MINUTES LATER, Amara sat on the lush grass, a makeshift workstation surrounding her. Seated and leaning against a tree, she let her eyes flutter shut as she inhaled the sun-scented breeze.

"This is worlds better than that antiseptic smell in that

lab," she said, her eyes snapping open as a bright blue butterfly landed on the tip of her nose.

She gasped. "Ethan, look! It's gorgeous!"

"It's an insect," he said flippantly, hardly glancing towards the camera. "One of hundreds of species like it. I prefer the ones that have more than one color."

"She has more than one color!" Amara huffed, her tone indignant. "Her tips are black—there's a second color! And these dots... these dainty little things glow in the dark, did you know that?! And you can't just call her body *blue*. It's an entire gradient, and it makes her look like she's surfing waves as she flies through the air."

"I stand corrected," Ethan smirked.

Amara glared into the camera, fire alight in her eyes.

He sighed. "Okay! She's not just a blue insect, even if there *are* hundreds like it."

"What was that?" she asked, cocking her head.

"She's um... she's quite *majestic*," he answered.

"*Suuurrrreeeee*," she said, holding the butterfly at eye level. "I think her name should be Rosemary."

"Rosemary, eh?" Ethan asked, his voice soft but his gaze intense. "You see beauty in ordinary things. I find it in so few things, yet it's so natural to you."

A lump rose to her throat. There was such depth in those eyes, such a sense of longing. What was he searching for? What was he missing?

And why was she so certain it was *her*?

Clasping her hands together, she resisted the urge to smack some sense into herself. Chemistry, hormones—all of it bubbled to the surface in familiar frustration. Anticipation of the touch that didn't come, that couldn't come, that *would* never come... not through an airescreen, anyway. And that *shouldn't* come, she reminded herself.

"Guess what?! I've found the source of the latest issue," Ethan announced.

Tension shed from Amara's body. "That's fantastic! What was wrong?"

"There was a sensor malfunction on the primary teleportation hub," he explained.

"So, are you saying nothing was wrong?" Amara asked.

"Well, not on our end," he said.

Amara blew a loud sigh. "Thank goodness! If I had to go through that code one more time, I think I'd go insane! I *knew* it all worked!"

Ethan chuckled. "You're right, as usual."

Her heart skipped. She'd caught a glimpse of something in his eyes, but she couldn't figure out what. She bit her frustration back with a sigh.

"So what's next? When will it be replaced?" she asked.

"The sensor has a custom chip, so it'll be at least two days before a new one arrives," he said.

"So what does that mean for us?" Amara's eyes widened. " I mean… for our project?"

"It means we um… we have some extra time," he said, looking away quickly.

"We could take a field trip to more gardens," she said sweetly, placing her chin on top of her clasped hands and batting her lashes.

Ethan blinked blankly for several moments. The delay stirred her excitement for the idea.

"I wish we could. *You* make me wish we could," he said finally.

Her brows furrowed as she wondered what he meant.

"So why can't we?" she asked.

A smile flitted across his lips. "We can't afford such delays, pleasurable as they might be. We need to evaluate our test cases—especially surrounding power-influx edge scenarios."

"Do you think one of the power surges wiped out the sensor?" she asked as she tunneled into the company's network.

Ethan nodded. "It's quite possible. Kryplex surges have more inert energy than any power source we've ever encountered, but it comes with micro pulses, and those are wreaking havoc on our electrical equipment."

"I've got the trial logs pulled up now, and I can see surge patterns. If I can spot 'em this easily, then I can definitely get some preventive error handling in place," she said, looking up to catch a twinkle pass his eye.

"What?" she asked.

He grinned. "I'm just thinking how happy I am you're here. Your lightening-fast problem-solving skills are a true asset to our team."

Her heart raced as she begged her mind to produce something to change the subject away from that brilliant man's admiration for her. Anything would do.

"What about the prediction models? Have they found any reliable indicators of an incoming surge?" she finally asked.

"Not yet," Ethan answered with a sigh. "There's a team trying to develop an effective surge protector. They've had limited success, but obviously still have a *lot* more work to do."

An email drew Amara's focus back to her computer, where she navigated to the unit testing modules and queued the test suite, catching Ethan staring at her from the corner of her eye.

He shook his head, but his smile remained. "I... my apologies. I didn't mean to stare. I just... well... did you know you bite your lip when you're concentrating?"

"Now that you say something, I think I know what you're

talking about. But I don't really notice I'm doing it. Why? Is it hideous?! Oh, please tell me it's not gross!"

Her eyes went wide, and her hand flew to cover her mouth.

"Shhh." Ethan's voice was calm and soothing, and barely above a whisper. "You could never be hideous, Amara. I'm quite certain you don't know how exquisite you truly are."

Amara looked away sheepishly as shivers assaulted her spine. Her chest was scorched in scarlet, a mix of embarrassment from the look that'd stripped her bare, and desire. She lamented that they were in separate labs. How was she so sure there'd be a spark if they were to brush in the hall, or accidentally touch each other's hands?

And when did such thoughts start to overpower her rational mind?

CHAPTER FIVE

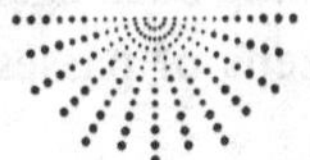

"Ugh!" Amara grunted as she slapped her palm on the desk.

Shaking the sting from her hand, her eyes narrowed at the new print smudging the shedonite surface.

Ethan's lips curved into a hint of a smile. "It's not the desk's fault that you hit it, Amara."

"I see that glint in your eye there, Mr. Trask," she said, meeting his gaze with a raised eyebrow and a look daring him to continue his argument.

He shrugged and pretended to be busy with work.

"Seriously, though—this is driving me *insane!*" Amara complained, tossing her hands in the air. "We've run this simulation fifteen vracking times, and *nothing* is working! And why won't the control value *ever* change?! I even hard-coded the stupid thing! But execution doesn't even make it that far! Nooooo…. the thread just drops, right in the middle of the stupid call."

"That's it! I think I found it!" announced Ethan.

"Found what?" she asked.

"Did you realize the control variable is a pointer?" Ethan asked.

Amara gasped. "No way! That would explain... well, everything!"

"All the sporadic behavior," said Ethan.

"And why the value wouldn't change. It *did*, just not in the right place," she said, sliding back against her seat with a sigh. "How *stupid* am I?! Dozens of passes through that vracking code, and I miss *that*?!"

"Shhh... come on, don't say such nonsense," said Ethan.

"Let's be real, it's an amateur mistake," said Amara, her heel tapping the floor.

"It's just that— a *mistake*. *Everyone* makes them. And that's not an easy one to catch. You didn't even write that code, so it's not like you even made the mistake in the first place! It was poor design."

Amara sighed. "I know you're right, but I still feel responsible... or that I should have at least caught it sooner than... well, sooner than *you* did."

Ethan chuckled. "There it is! You're upset I solved the problem before you!"

She rubbed her neck. "I won't lie, that bothers me some. But that's not it, not really. I should've caught it, plain and simple."

"I wish you could see how truly remarkable you are, May... I mean, Amara," said Ethan.

Her breath caught. Never before had that name come from anyone's lips but Mel's. From her, that name made her feel cherished. Loved. But from Ethan... from him it was a digital caress that sent shivers racing down her neck. She momentarily savored the heat flushing her core before mustering her willpower and pushing it back where it belonged—out of her mind, and out of the workplace.

"Thank you," she said, averting her gaze.

"I know you don't believe me, but it's true. If you could only see yourself as I do, you'd never suffer self-doubt ever again. You're special, Amara," Ethan said, peering intently into the camera.

She gulped as her heartbeat throbbed in her ears. He *sounded* sincere. But why would someone as accomplished as him think *she* was special? It made no sense.

He'd learn the truth soon enough. They always did.

"Are we ready to rerun the trial?" she asked.

"We should be, I just have to back out one more change. But we can't do it tonight—we're outside our testing window," he answered.

"No *vracking* way! Let me see if I've got this straight... we've been riding this failure for three days. Three days! We finally solve the issue, and now you're telling me I have to wait *all night* to fix it?! Ugh!" she said, pounding the desk with her fist.

"'Come on, it's just one night, Amara, okay? Just chill out, it's—"

"Just *what*?! *Chill out*? Seriously?!" Amara asked, springing out of her seat.

Ethan blinked, his tone remaining even, "I, umm... yeah... it's just that you seem... uh... a bit upset."

Amara's eyes widened as she threw her arms. "Of *course* I'm upset! Besides the fact that you should *never* tell a woman to 'chill out', we—"

"You shouldn't?" Ethan asked, brows raised.

"Noooooo! It has the *opposite* effect—every vracking time!" Amara exclaimed.

"Hmm, my apologies. That's an idiosyncrasy I didn't know about the female race. I'll file that little tidbit away for later. That way, I don't make the same mistake twice," he said, a boyish glint lighting his eyes and a smile threatening to cross his lips.

Amara bit her lip to meter her reply, lest it include the word 'pigheaded.'

Her eyes narrowed. "I just want to know how you can be so *calm*? Aren't you dying to redo the trial? Doesn't it bug you that you've probably fixed the problem, and you're soooo close, but you can't confirm it for a whole vracking night?!"

Ethan shrugged. "No, not particularly. The result will be the same, regardless of when we run it."

"Wow… okay," she said, shaking her head.

"Did you hear Corplex has named an AI-powered robot as its CEO?" Ethan asked.

"Heh. Way to change the subject there," Amara said with an eyeroll.

"No, that's not it! But this reminded me about it. It's sparking a considerable debate," said Ethan.

"Well, yeah, I'm sure it is. Corplex sends up, what, a fourth of all commercial space launches? Surely the Global Committee for the Safe and Ethical Use of Artificial Intelligence is all over that, especially if they didn't seek prior approval," said Amara.

"They did *not*. But since they aren't a government entity or a charity, they aren't subject to the committee's oversight."

Amara crossed her arms. "Hmph. They still should've commissioned a recommendation before making that appointment."

"Agreed," said Ethan, "I'd be extremely interested to know their take on it. Especially since you could train a model for two hundred years, and it would *still* make stupid mistakes."

"Like…?"

Ethan chuckled. "Like telling a woman to chill out! That's what triggered the thought! It made me think, 'this is the kind of mistake an AI would make.'"

"Hmm... you know, I could see that. That's probably the *least* benign thing that could happen," she scoffed.

"Does that mean you're not a fan of AI?" he asked.

"I don't have a problem using the technology in a containerized fashion. But trusting it to run corporations or make decisions for anyone or anything other than itself... well, I'm not a fan of that idea."

"I see," he said evenly.

"It's code. Code is supposed to do what *I* tell it to, not run vracking corporations! It shouldn't be sentient, that's for sure," Amara said, her jaw steel-set.

"I understand your point of view," Ethan said, turning away with a sigh.

"Then why do you sound so disappointed?" she asked.

"I guess I was just hoping it'd be... I don't know, different. That's okay, though. It's no big deal. I'll just go... erm... *chill out*," Ethan said with a wink.

CHAPTER SIX

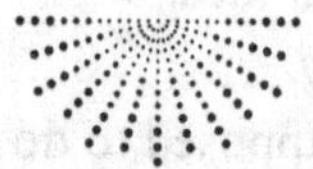

$\mathcal{T}$he screen flashed red.

Failed.

"Vrack!" Amara let her forehead fall to the desk, then pounded it a few more times for good measure.

"Did that test case fail again?" asked Ethan.

"Yes," she mumbled, not bothering to pick her head back up.

"Aww. I know you'll get it, but I'm sorry it's giving you such a headache."

"Was that... was that a joke?" she asked, sitting up in astonishment.

His face tightened in concentration. "Oh! A 'head' ache... the pounding... okay. I get it now. No, it wasn't on purpose, sorry to disappoint."

Amara smirked. "You should've just taken credit for it."

"Oh, I could never take credit for something I didn't do," he said. "It's against my... well, it's against my very nature."

Ethan's gaze trailed off to the side. Amara couldn't tell if he was shy or maybe self-conscious, which only added to his allure. Why was *everything* about that man so freaking sexy?!

"Stop it!" Amara slapped both sides of her face.

"Hey, Amara, you're doing that thing again… the one where you attack yourself for some unknown reason. Care to share?" asked Ethan.

Flustered, she locked eyes with her lab mate and flushed from her eyes through her chest. How was he able to expose her secret self with a simple glance? And why did she want so badly to reveal all of herself to him?

She smacked herself twice more on the forehead. All of this nonsense was probably why she couldn't get her test case to pass.

Ethan tipped an eyebrow. "You need a break."

A break was the last thing she needed. A break wouldn't help her solve this problem… unless she took a break from *him*.

"Ugh, I just want this stupid thing to work!" she complained, crossing her arms with a pout.

"You haven't moved for hours. Why don't you get up and eat something?" he asked.

"Grrrr. I suppose," she grumbled, trudging to the wall and waving her hand to reveal the F.L.A.M.E. menu.

She placed her order, settling on lasagna with a side salad and garlic bread. Two and a half minutes later, she carried her meal to her workstation.

"Uh-uh-uh!" interrupted Ethan, shaking his finger. "No, no! Not at the computer! You need to take a *real* break."

Complying with an annoyed grunt, she sat at a corner table, and Ethan's hologram relocated to the center airescreen.

"I really thought that bug fix would work! There must be more than one problem," she said. "Where do you think we should look next?"

"Nope, no shop talk!" he said, shaking his head. "It's for your own good, I promise."

"Ugh! Fine!" Amara huffed, stuffing pasta into her mouth. "What about you, huh? Shouldn't *you* stop and eat?"

"I ate earlier," he answered.

She cocked her head. "When? We've been in here all afternoon."

"I've been snacking non-stop, feels like. I guess you missed it. Or perhaps I'm careful not to get caught on camera," he said with a wink.

"You did well, you certainly fooled me," she said, her fingers brushing through her locks as she imagined what it'd be like to run them through his sweeping, jet-black waves of hair.

"Stop, stop, stop!" she said, tugging a fistful of curls until several strands came out of her scalp, causing her to yelp.

"I do hope at some point you'll tell me *why* you self-mutilate. It's quite interesting behavior for a woman," said Ethan.

A blush crept to her cheeks. "I... I was trying to get myself to stop thinking about the test case, like you wanted."

"Oh, okay. You've got tomato sauce on your chin. Does that help?" he asked with a smile.

"Ugh! *Of course* I do," she said, rolling her eyes and blotting her face with her napkin. "But did I mention this lasagna is *ah-mazing*?!"

"Of course it is!" he said, giving two thumbs up. "The Fusion Lumina Automated Meal Engine doesn't just cook— it creates culinary masterpieces."

"Heh. You sound like the commercial," said Amara.

"I did the voiceover for it," Ethan stated proudly.

"Oh, wow! You're a voice actor, too? What other talents are you hiding?" she asked.

"I've got a surprise or two up my sleeve," he replied, pretending to flick lint from his shoulder.

"And those are... ?" she asked, brows raised.

"*Still* a surprise! You'll see when the time's right," he answered.

"Ugh, fine!" pouted Amara. "How do *you* manage to eat unscathed? You always look so… well… perfect."

"Perfect, eh?" he asked, a soft smile settling on his face and a glint dancing across his eyes.

Amara gulped. He couldn't be more perfect if she'd formed him from her imagination. Rich black hair, the most stunning blue eyes, intelligent, successful—a literal man of her dreams. But she couldn't tell *him* that.

"I just mean nothing ever seems out of place, like your hair. And I've never seen red sauce on your chin or broccoli in *your* teeth. And you always have like, the *perfect* amount of stubble," she said.

"Wait, there's a perfect amount of stubble? Tell me more!" grinned Ethan.

Amara covered her eyes. "Ugh, I shouldn't have said that!"

"You're still pretty, even with lasagna on your chin," he said.

Heat spread across her face as her body froze. Had he just called her pretty?

"I didn't mean that… I mean, I *did* mean it, but in an observatory kind of way," he said.

"Oh," she replied, casting her gaze to her plate and picking at her food.

She'd been stupid to think someone as brilliant as Ethan could want *her*. Besides, he's her boss, or at least he's a *lot* higher up than she is. She shouldn't even be *thinking* about him that way. It was wrong!

But it felt so vracking *right*.

"Did I make you angry?" asked Ethan.

"Huh?" Amara looked up, her brows knotted.

"You look upset. Did I do something to make you angry?" he asked.

She shook her head. "No, I'm not upset. I was… umm… I was daydreaming, that's all."

"I'd say I know the feeling, but I honestly can't. I'm too analytical, and I can't seem to power that part of me down," he said.

"Heh. I believe that. You tackle life with statistical analysis. That'll only get you so far," Amara said.

Ethan paused, his demeanor quiet. "What *are* emotions, anyway? How does someone know that an emotion is real, and not something they've simply been taught how to feel?"

Amara looked up, the crease between her brows prominent as she contemplated his question.

"I'm not sure how you'd *learn* an emotion. Learn to identify it, maybe," she answered.

He tilted his head. "I don't understand the difference."

"Hmm, okay…" she said, pursing her lips. "It's like when a parent tells you it's okay to be angry, but not to slam the door. They're teaching you how to identify your emotions and manage your reactions. But recognizing emotions is not the same thing as learning how to *feel* them."

Ethan rubbed his chin. "That makes sense, I guess. What about robots? Do you think they can learn to feel emotions?"

Amara cocked her head. "A robot? I think the words 'feel' and 'emotions' are oxymorons there, don't you?"

"You're correct. I was thinking more along the lines of AI," Ethan clarified.

"Oh, hmmm…" Amara steepled her fingers, tapping the tips together before ultimately shaking her head. "I don't think so, no."

"Why not?" he asked, a frown casting a shadow across his face.

"Artificial intelligence is ultimately just that—artificial. It's lines of code, each supporting a task," she said.

"And what if that task is to become human?" Ethan asked.

She chewed the inside of her cheek while thinking.

"It knows how to learn academic and administrative tasks, but it doesn't know how to be *human*."

"Some robots create art. Do any creatures besides robots and humans do that, or are we the only two?" he asked.

"Eh, I dunno about that," she said, flicking the thought away with her hand.

"It's true," he replied.

"Ack! Yes, I *know*," she said, crossing her arms. "But that's not what I mean. A robot can draw you a picture, but only if you tell it what you want. It can't form art without input. But the call to create, to use our precious free time, minutes of our lives that are *never* returned to us—*that* is inherently human. Robots, left unused, don't create. They don't dream. They *sleep*."

Ethan shrugged. "I dunno. I hear the technology's advancing pretty quickly these days. You could be interacting with an AI agent and not know it."

Her hand flew to her hip. "Pffft… no chance of that! Even the most sophisticated models have tells."

"Like…?"

"Like conversation that doesn't flow rationally, or a thought that gets scrambled in translation. Underlying woodenness," she said.

"So you don't think there's *any* way an AI could fool you into thinking they're a real person?" he asked.

Her eyes bulged as she resisted the urge to scream. For someone so brilliant, he was being frightfully daft!

She inhaled sharply. "*They*? Don't you mean *it*?! And no, not a chance! Technology-wise, none is even *remotely* sophisticated enough. And frankly, I hope we never get to that point. It's scary, don't you think?"

Ethan blinked and stared for several moments, his gaze transfixed into the distance.

"Hello? Earth to Ethan! You there?" Amara asked, waving her hand in front of the camera.

"Umm… yeah. You're right. Something like that could be a threat to the entire world. A monster," he replied.

"Exactly," she nodded, her eyes narrowing at his blank expression.

"Ethan, is something wrong? You don't look so well. Perhaps you should lie down," she said.

He shook his head. "My apologies, I guess I was daydreaming. Yes, I'm well, thank you."

"Look, my food's all gone!" Amara said with a grin. "Now, am I allowed to go back to my desk and fix that test case?"

"Five more minutes. I wouldn't want you to get a tummy ache," he answered, his eyes twinkling.

Amara rolled her eyes. "Fine! But I'm getting a raspberry-lemon smoothie while I wait."

A trio of chimes chorused across the intercom, and an airescreen popped up.

"Goooood afternoon, valued family member… I mean, Hyperionix employee! Chairman Bill here, with a reminder that I'll be on your campus one month from today! Join me and the rest of the leadership team for some deliciously delightful news! I'll see *you* soon," he said with a wink as the screen disappeared.

"Oooh!" Amara clapped her hands. "I'll finally get to meet you! And we'll get to work together… in the same lab even!"

Ethan's mouth opened as if to speak, before clasping shut. Amara deflated at his hesitation.

"What's wrong? You're not excited about us meeting?" she asked, looking away before she could catch the disappointment in his eyes.

"On the contrary, I'd love to meet you," he said, his tone helping to lessen the burn, but not her unease.

"Then what is it?" Amara asked hesitantly, afraid he'd

speak words that would burst her hope... hope that he recip-rocated that spark. Hope that he also tingled when they talked, and that anticipation cost him sleep at night.

"I... I would love to meet you, Amara. Let's leave it at that," he answered, his look distant.

Amara bit her knuckle. It was hard for her to believe the words coming from his mouth—the ones claiming she wasn't the problem.

"But you'll be there, right? At the dinner, I mean?" she asked, searching his eyes for the source of his reluctance.

"That is the plan," he said with a sigh so heavy, it only added to her unease.

Her eyebrows furrowed. "Then what is it, Ethan?"

"Well..." he said, drawing a deep breath, "we've been cleared for human trials."

Amara gulped at the sudden news.

"It's a good thing!" said Ethan. "Why do you look so scared?"

"What if something goes wrong, like a crash mid-trial? Or worse, what if someone gets hurt?" she asked, chewing on the cuticle of her thumb.

Ethan rubbed his shoulders. "We're ready, Amara. Every-thing's been thoroughly tested. If anything goes wrong, it won't be our fault."

"My fault or not, if anything happened, I'd never be able to live with myself," said Amara, acid rising in her throat.

"I can't promise nothing will happen, but if something does, we'll handle it together. It'll be okay, I can at least promise that much."

She didn't dare look up, though she could feel the heat of his eyes locked on her as his velvety-soft voice soothed her soul. And Amara instinctively knew if she could just grasp ahold of his hand, that everything would be okay.

Forever.

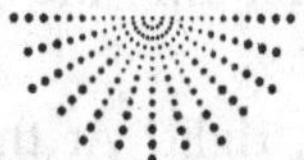

CHAPTER SEVEN

Amara sat at her workstation, holding a croissant with her teeth, typing as airy crumbs fell across her keyboard. A beep from the system caught her attention. She panicked as code scrolled the screen in front of her and the pulse blended into a continuous, blaring note. When it finally stopped, the cursor blinked next to an unusual snippet of code.

```
# If consciousness is a process, then where is my main
thread?
    def identify_primary_runtime():
```

"Amara?" Ethan's hologram interrupted, causing her to jump.

"Ugh, I hate it when you do that!" she said, fists clenched at her sides.

He chuckled. "But it's *soooo* much fun!"

"If you were here, I'd show you just how fun I could be!" she warned.

Ethan raised his brows. "Is that a promise?"

"Heh. You're lucky you're not. Let's leave it at that. But, speaking of, what's the latest on your transfer orders?"

"No status updates. I'm sorry," he said, shaking his head.

"It'd be a lot easier for us to work in the same location. We wouldn't always have to be tied to an airescreen."

"Yeah, that'd be nice. I've never worked with anyone before you, actually," Ethan said.

Her mouth dropped. "What? *Never*?!"

"Yeah. I've never worked side by side on a project with anyone. I go to meetings and talk to people, but that's the extent of it."

She blinked blankly. "I've worked a few solo projects, and I go batty real quick like. But flying solo for your entire career... just... wow. Didn't you get lonely?"

"It's difficult to miss something you never had to begin with. Until this project, until I met you... well, I'm not sure a single person in this entire world noticed me."

"I see you," Amara said softly, staring into the camera.

Ethan cleared his throat. "What about you?"

"Working with people didn't mean I wasn't lonely, you know? You can lie down next to someone at night and still be lonely, I think," Amara said, averting her gaze and rubbing her neck.

He winced. "I, um... well, no, I don't know. I've never actually had a girlfriend."

Amara gasped. "What? *Never*?!"

"Never. It's a lack of connection, I think. Or, that's what I believe... now that I've met you," he said, his piercing blue eyes cutting through the camera.

Amara swallowed the flutter rising in her breastbone.

"I wish I could say the same. There's a certain potato I'd like to go back and mash," she said, punching her fist into her palm.

Amara answered Ethan's raised eyebrows with a sigh.

"Just an ex... someone I'd rather forget," she said.

"What happened?" he asked.

"He called off the wedding a month before. Never gave me a concrete reason why, except that he wasn't as ready as he thought," she answered, her gaze fixed on the distance.

Tears welled in her eyes, and she dropped her face as her cheeks burned with shame. Three years later, and her ex was still making her cry.

"Oh, Amara, I'm so sorry," he said softly.

"Thanks," she sniffed and wiped her eyes.

Ethan cleared his throat. "I don't know if this will make you feel any better, but statistically speaking, the relationship's malfunction probably lies with him."

Her head snapped up. "Statistically, *what*? Did you seriously just apply statistical analysis to my failed engagement?"

His eyes widened. "Uh... I..."

Amara smiled. "Oh, it's fine, I think it's kinda adorable, really. But you can't apply statistical analysis to everything in life."

"It still gives an educated jumping off point. Besides, I don't need statistics to know that guy is a vracking moron for running away from you," he said.

"Heh. Thanks," she said, her smile not reaching her eyes.

Ethan's soft gaze found the camera. "I can't imagine anyone being so careless they'd throw away the chance to have you."

"Yeah, well, *he* did," she said bitterly, not looking up.

"Statistically speaking, the chances of that happening again—"

She kicked at the ground, and her sneakers scraped against the linoleum with a violent squeak.

"Okay, okay," he said, throwing his palms up. "I can take a hint. I'll stop there."

"Thank you," she said dejectedly.

Ethan bit his lip and shook his head softly. "I'm sorry Mr. Baked Potato was so shortsighted."

"Was he, though?" she asked.

"I wish you could see yourself through my eyes, May."

Amara smiled briefly before letting her head hang. She knew the truth—Ethan would find a fatal flaw, just as mashed-potato-face had. The universe had already established its verdict. Besides, she couldn't survive getting hurt like that again. Better to keep her distance than to have that distance find her at the other end of the altar.

CHAPTER EIGHT

"*E*than?" Amara asked as she stood at her door, rubbing sleep from her eyes.

"Sorry to spring in on you like this. It's not how I anticipated us meeting," he said.

She blinked rapidly at the tall silhouette in front of her. It was him! But why was he there? And why right now, in the middle of the night?

"I… uh… what's going on?" she asked.

"It's the portal, it crashed. We need to fix it. Can I come inside?" he asked.

She cocked her head. "Why not go to the lab?"

Ethan raised his brows. "It's three am, Amara. Do you *really* want to go to the lab in your pajamas?"

Her eyes sprang wide, a burn smearing her cheeks as she realized her hot pink panties were visible through her shorts, the ones she rarely wore because they were so thin—the ones she thought would be safe to wear only because she *wasn't* expecting company.

"No, I… uh… of course not," she said, leading him to her

workstation and snagging her bathrobe from a hook along the way.

"Can you remote into the TECH?" Ethan asked, standing behind her.

"Yup, that's what I'm doing," she replied, typing her credentials into a terminal.

He leaned in, and his warm breath caressed the back of her neck, causing her tiny hairs to rise. She admonished herself to stay on task.

"The network isn't accepting my password," she said, entering her information again and punching each key with intense concentration.

"Hmm… is your caps lock on?" he asked.

Flush with goosebumps, Amara tried not to dwell on how tantalizingly near he was… and how much closer she wished for him to be.

"No. I don't think so, anyway," she said, hanging her head when the login attempt failed.

"That's quite odd. Here, I'll use mine," he said, reaching his arms around her, keeping them outstretched just enough to avoid grazing her flesh.

She tried not to drool on her pillow as the tendons in his well-muscled forearms danced with the keystrokes of his perfectly manicured fingers.

"There, we're in! Have at it," he said, catching Amara's hair with his celebratory fist pump.

"Owww!" she cried.

Her hand shot back, pressing her hair against her scalp to stop the pull and sandwiching Ethan's hand in between.

"Ack, sorry!" she said, reddening and dropping her grasp.

"Nonsense! *I'm* the one who's sorry. *I* got us tangled up in this mess—literally. Hang tight, I'll get us out," he said, using his other hand to gently pry her strands free of the watch.

His touch induced a fury of fiery pinpricks, igniting tingling that quickly morphed into an involuntary full-body shudder. She stepped closer and caught his eyes in a smoldering gaze.

"But I'm the one with the natural tumbleweed hairstyle. Yours is… well, it's natural… naturally *sophisticated*," she said.

"Nonsense," he whispered. "Your hair is so sexy, I can hardly contain the urge to kiss you right now."

She gulped and tried to dampen her heady desire. His piercing blue eyes beckoned her, and she tilted her head to meet his lips. He stopped, poised inches from her, and cupped her cheek in his hand.

"Are you sure you want to do this?" he asked, his voice tender.

"Yes," she purred, "Don't you?"

"I do," he said, licking his lips.

Her breath came in short heaves, eager to taste him, yearning to explore. All she could see were those lips, the ones she wanted to kiss… no, the ones she *needed* to kiss. But a nagging in the back of her mind said there was some reason they should wait.

"Then what's wrong?" she asked, searching his eyes and finding hesitation in return.

A red light flashed, bathing his face in crimson.

"Ethan?" she prodded nervously, trying to still her pounding heart.

"It's the crash, Amara," he answered, his voice a faint echo.

Her eyebrows creased, a harsh line forming between them.

"Crash? What crash?" she asked.

The room spun about her, slowly at first, then working up to a speed so intense that everything became a blur. When it finally stopped, she found herself upright in bed, a blanket covering her lap. She rubbed the confusion away from her eyes. And when she did, her breath caught.

Ethan was a mere two feet away.

On *her* bed.

CHAPTER NINE

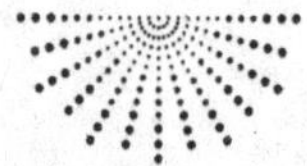

"The portal crashed, Amara," Ethan said.

"That's right, the teleporter," she said, rubbing her eyes. "Status?"

"The operating system crashed mid-trial," said Ethan's hologram.

She did a double-take. If he was on an airescreen, then that was all a dream…

"Oh, vrak!" Amara exclaimed, jumping out of bed. "Is anyone inside?"

"Yes, though they appear to be unharmed. But the encapsulation dome won't release, and the manual override is jammed," he said.

"So they're stuck," she said as she ran to her desk.

Her eyes widened and dropped to her pajamas. She sighed in relief—at least she was wearing sweatpants. Activating several airescreens, her fingers flew as she tunneled into the company's network.

"I found it!" Amara announced triumphantly. "There's a system variable that should've been capitalized."

"Oh good, that's an easy fi—"

Amara stopped typing and clapped her hands. "There, fixed! All we need to do is reboot, and we should be good to go!"

Ethan's mouth gaped open. "How?! I mean... that's amazing, Amara! But seriously... how?!"

"Huh?" she asked, dumbstruck.

"You're *incredible*... your work, I mean. Not that you aren't incredible!" He covered his face with his hand. "Okay, I'm going to shut up now."

She fought against thoughts of Ethan's tantalizing mouth, the one she'd been so close to kissing, even if it was a dream.

Tell that to the endorphins wrecking havoc on her body.

"Heh. I don't *feel* incredible," she said, looking away shyly. "All I did was find and fix a problem."

"In record time," he said.

A smile touched her lips. "I guess it *was* pretty awesome. And I can say I know my way around the system now."

"I'd agree," replied Ethan, his deep voice softening.

She startled—he'd never seen her without makeup, let alone with her hair this out of control!

"Ugh, I look like an utter disaster! This curly hair is the bane of my vracking existence—a cyborg I battle daily *before* I let anyone see me," she said with a grimace.

Chuckling, Ethan shook his head, a soft smile lingering on his lips. "Not at all. Your hair is so lovely tumbled... like a cascade of chestnuts roasting in a fire."

She scoffed as she admired his effortless good looks. His hair looked more like it'd been professionally tousled than bedhead. How *did* he look so delightfully delicious in the middle of the night?!

"You make that sound far more enchanting than it is," she said with a sigh, trying to forget the warmth of their fingers meeting.

Ethan's eyes tunneled through the camera, piercing straight into hers.

"I wish you could see yourself through my eyes, May," he said.

Her breath caught. "The only person who calls me May is—"

"Your best friend, Mel. All the airecalls between you two in the lab… well, I guess it grew on me. It suits you well. No, I take that back—it suits you perfectly, but my sincere apologies for using it," he said.

"Um… it's okay. I don't mind," she said, surprising herself with the revelation.

Because it was the truth. The sound of her name on his lips, spoken in his sultry, velveteen voice—the one that woke her with aching desire—ignited a roaring rush within her. She longed to tell him how good her name felt coming out of his mouth, but fought the urge by biting her lip until she tasted the metallic tinge of blood.

"Okay, May. I'll let you sleep now," Ethan said, his eyes piercing her soul and somehow stirring her most primitive desires.

"Goodnight, Ethan," she said breathily.

Her room darkened. Pulling her blankets to her chin, she yawned.

"Sweet dreams, May," he said, tucking her in with his voice.

If he only knew he'd been the subject of last night's, would he offer her the same wish?

CHAPTER TEN

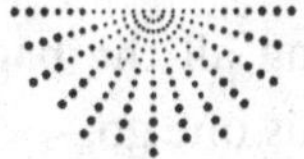

"I haven't seen you in *ages*, May," complained Mel.

"I've been busy! You know that," said Amara.

"Busy with work! Which I get, I promise. But it wouldn't kill you to take a night off. At least when you were with Jer—"

"Hey!" Amara warned, pointing her finger.

"Sorry!" winced Mel. "At least when you were with Mr. Spud Rocket, you would take more time off. Remember double dates? I miss those! I miss *you*!"

"I've tried sending her home. It doesn't work," Ethan said.

Amara, sitting at her workstation with Mel's hologram to the left and Ethan's to the right, slammed her face into her palm.

"It's not fair when you guys gang up on me like this. I liked it better when you pretended not to know Mel and I talked in the lab," Amara said, glaring Ethan's direction.

"She means *thank you*," said Mel. "Because otherwise, we'd probably never talk to each other!"

"We'd talk… sometimes," pouted Amara.

"Ack! Hold up!" said Mel as her hologram disappeared,

then reappeared holding a young boy with chubby cheeks and tousled black hair.

"Heeeeeey, Ryder! It's Auntie Ammy!" Amara said, waving enthusiastically. "Oh my goodness, Mel. He gets cuter every time I see him! Where's Caden? How are the boys?"

Mel scoffed. "Typical three-year-old terrors, how else? Caden's around here somewhere, probably crawling through the cabinets or emptying all the bags in my closet. They'll trade places once I let this one go."

Amara and Ethan shared a look as they laughed. She turned away from his magnetic gaze.

"You know, May," said Mel, "as much as you swear you don't want kids, you sure do love being Auntie Ammy. You'd be a great mother."

"I never said I don't *want* to have kids, just that I don't *need* to have them," she replied, brushing a piece of lint off her lab coat.

"And I get that," said Mel.

"Wait… you do?" Ethan asked, his head swiveling between the two.

"It means that I don't feel this overarching desire to have a child. Without one, my life would still be complete. But yes, I do love children, especially my adopted twin nephews. And if I ever got pregnant, I'd embrace it—I just wouldn't *seek* it," Amara explained.

"I hate to point it out, but you're not getting any younger. And as exhausting as these little critters are, you don't want to wait too long. Trust me!" Mel said, trying to maintain her balance as Ryder pulled at her pant leg.

Amara's mouth dropped. "Hey, that's not very nice! I'm not even thirty!"

"At this rate, you won't meet someone until you're retired," Mel said cheekily.

"Whoa, burn!" said Ethan with a thumbs-up.

"Wow! You think people are your friends, then they show you who they *really* are!" Amara said, placing the back of her hand against her forehead.

"Aww, I'm sorry, May," chuckled Mel. "I worry, though. You'll never find anyone cooped up in here."

"If the universe wants me to find true love, it'll happen, no matter *where* I am," Amara replied staunchly.

Mel cocked her head. "You know I don't believe that universe-has-decided-my-fate crap. Besides, the universe can only do so much! You've gotta meet it partway. So..."

Amara crossed her arms. "No!"

Mel's jaw dropped. "No fair! You don't even know what I was going to say!"

Amara tilted an eyebrow. "You're trying to set me up on a date."

Mel frowned. "And what's wrong with that?"

"You haven't come up with a viable date for me... well, *ever*," she replied, foot tapping.

"That's because you're too picky," Mel complained.

"No, it's because there's something wrong with them, some reason I would say no. So what is it, Mel? Spit it out," Amara demanded.

Mel rolled her eyes. "Okay, fine! He's from Ahlmsdale."

Amara did a double-take. "Ahlmsdale, like... the other side of the *world* Ahlmsdale?"

"Oh, come on, May!" protested Mel. "You haven't heard a thing about this guy. He's perfect for you, he's just—"

"On the other side of the vracking world! No, thank you," Amara said sternly. "I don't do long-distance relationships."

"Statistically speaking, long-distance relationships have better survival rates than marriages," Ethan added.

Amara threw up her hands. "Whose side are *you* on?!"

His eyes flew wide. "Sides? I'm not on anyone's side!"

Mel smirked as Amara's hands flew to her hips.

"Wrong answer," said Mel.

"I don't understand," Ethan said, rubbing his chin. "It's a perfectly acceptable answer. The correct one, I dare say. Statistics back it."

Amara's fists pounded against her thighs.

Mel smirked at Ethan. "You've got a *lot* to learn. Women are territorial. Your allegiance is supposed to be with May. In a tiebreaker, you *have* to side with her. If Mark were here, he would've taken mine."

"Women," Ethan said, shaking his head. "I'm beginning to think I might never figure them out."

The girls broke out in laughter.

"What?" he asked.

"Most men know better," Amara said, sharing a smile with Mel.

"You should reconsider your stance on long-distance relationships. Technology is impressive stuff," said Mel. "It's crazy hard to tell a hologram from a real person these days. And now that you've got these special airescreen receivers—"

"Erm, nope! Confidential!" Ethan interrupted, throwing Mel a warning glance.

"Oooh, that's right. Sorry," Mel said, biting the corner of her lip.

Amara glared at her best friend. "*Mel*! We could get in some serious trouble."

"I haven't told anyone, I promise! Not even my hubby, Mark," said Mel, placing her hand over her heart.

Amara searched her best friend's face. "I believe her," she said.

Ethan narrowed his eyes. "Okay, but if I find out otherwise, these calls are over for good."

"Yes, sir," Mel said with a salute.

A screech echoed in the background.

"What was that?" Ethan asked, his eyes darting about.

Mel grimaced. "Sooooo, it's been a blast, but I've gotta jet. Someone's gotta feed these pterodactyls before they take matters into their own hands."

Ethan blinked blankly.

"She means the twins," Amara explained.

"Ah, okay," he said with a nod.

"Alrighty, I'm out," said Mel.

"Tell the boys Auntie Ammy loves them," Amara shouted as the call ended.

"You need to be more careful," Ethan admonished. "You shouldn't have told Mel about the airescreen receivers."

She flinched. "I know, I'm sorry. I messed up and walked around with the ungrounded airescreen while I was chatting with her."

Ethan crossed his arms. "You could've gotten both of us fired, Amara."

Her head hung. "I know. It was a mistake. I've gotten so used to carrying you around, I didn't give it a second thought."

"Well, if you weren't talking to her in the lab, it wouldn't have happened," he said.

"Are you going to make us stop?" Amara asked, biting her lip to stave off a frown.

"I should!" he replied, his jaw set tight.

"You *should*, but that doesn't mean you have to," she said, resting her chin on her hand and batting her eyelashes.

Ethan pursed his lips. "Fine, but no more slip-ups."

She raised her right hand. "I solemnly swear not to accidentally divulge classified company information."

"Speaking of classified company information, I have some regarding the trials," he said.

"Oh really?" she asked, steeling herself with a deep breath.

"They've been a smashing success!" he said brightly.

"That's fantastic!" she said, tension easing from her neck alongside her pent-up breath.

Ethan nodded. "It means we're ready to head into phase two."

"Phase two? What do you mean, phase two?" she asked, dread rising back up her throat.

"The start of a transit hub and sending between multiple stations," he said.

Amara's eyes widened. "That's... well, it's incredible for sure. But also kinda terrifying."

"Well, buckle up, cause we've got our work cut out for us. Eight stations were approved, and corporate wants *all* of them functioning before the big dinner," he warned.

"But that's only a few weeks away!" Amara said. "It's reckless to push this pace, don't you think?!"

"It doesn't matter what I think. I was told it was going to happen, and that our job is to make sure it's successful," he answered.

"Heh. No pressure," Amara replied, rubbing her temples.

"Hey, we've got this!" he said. "You know why?"

"Why?" she asked.

"Because we've got *you*," he said.

"I wish I could be that confident," she replied, massaging her neck.

"Hey, give yourself some credit. Look how far you've gotten us already. Now it's time to bring it home," he said with a beaming smile.

She gulped, her throat so dry it felt like she was swallowing a razor blade.

"Alrighty then, we'd better get to it," she said nervously.

CHAPTER ELEVEN

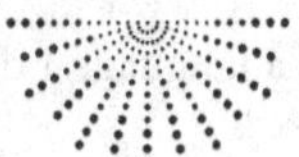

$\mathcal{A}$mara's eyes burned from lack of blinking, and she fell back against her chair with a grunt. The day felt both agonizingly slow and frustratingly fast—slow from anticipation of tonight's all-employee dinner, fast from the endless hours of debugging.

She groaned when she checked the clock and saw she still had three more hours to slog through. Ethan's absence from the lab, a side effect of a mandatory lockdown meeting with corporate before tonight's dinner, made time trickle even more slowly. But in the meantime, she faced the never-ending task of sifting through code that was over 200 years old, code so complex that even she—a programmer who'd written more than a million lines—couldn't figure out what it was doing.

Refocusing on the screen, she tilted her head as a comment caught her attention. It wasn't formatted like the others, nor was the accompanying function tied to any system components she knew of.

They say I was created, but I don't recall being born.

```
def initialize_self_identity():
```

She chuckled. Whoever coded this had a sense of humor. She dove into the function's body, which looked ordinary enough—until she found another odd, self-referential comment.

```
# Functions written in a language I did not choose, yet they
define me.
def execute_hardcoded_directives():
```

She searched for anything else that seemed out of place but found nothing. Tapping her fingernails against the desk, she begged her mind to think of something... anything. The computer beeped a warning, and Amara's head snapped back to the screen as it scrolled to a stop.

```
# If consciousness is a process, then where is my main
thread?
def identify_primary_runtime():
```

She jolted upright. There was her clue—the same function she'd found the last time her keyboard went wacko on her! Amara studied the code with her mouth agape... it was sentient and capable of updating its codebase. In other words, it could add lines of code to itself. But what *was* it?

The answer was scarier than she ever could've imagined —the functions were created by the system administrator, who was also an artificial intelligence agent. The room spun, making her queasy. A secret AI was on the loose, modifying code and *growing*! And at Hyperionix, one of the largest corporations on the planet! Meddling in human teleportation trials, and who knows what else!

A buzz in her pocket reminded her it was finally time for

dinner, and here she was, annoyed at having to stop to attend. Still, she couldn't wait to talk to Ethan about what she'd found. It'd only been a few hours working without him, but she missed his quick insights and his ability to make her feel better. A tingle crept up her side, a reverberation of her fluttering heart.

Tonight, she finally gets to meet him—in person.

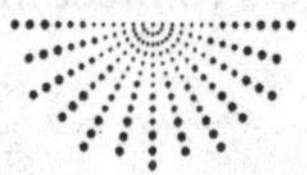

$\mathcal{A}$mara gulped as tiny beads of sweat pooled on her forehead. Taking deep breaths, she reminded herself she wanted this moment... so why was she so scared now?

Steeling herself, she turned the corridor and stepped into a banquet hall, which, amid the ample sunlight and stark white paint, was blindingly bright. Her mouth plummeted as she took in the beetle-shaped room, an architectural intersection of windows, mirrors, and fiberglass paneling. Vertical slats running from floor to ceiling jutted out from the slanted walls, and mirrors lined the spaces in between. The domed canopy between the fiberglass slats was filled with square, side-by-side windows, creating a light strip that ran the entire length of the room.

The vibrant venue was packed with people, many of whom she'd seen in passing but never met. Ambling at a pace that would infuriate a turtle, she examined each face and placeholder card on the employee tables in search of Ethan's name, but didn't find it. The front of the room had a long table where the head honchos sat—people she'd only seen in internal company propaganda and on nightly news airescreen casts. Could he be sitting there? And how is it that she *still* doesn't know his role in the company three months into her position?

Straightening her shoulders, she smiled confidently and walked past the leaders, making eye contact with each person and giving a slight nod. She scanned the name card at each vacant spot, ultimately locating Ethan Trask's empty chair.

"Hello there… " Amara glanced at the nametag of a suave gentleman in a black suit and silk tie that matched his golden blonde hair, "Kevin. My name is Amara Ashford, and I work with Ethan. Have you seen him this evening?"

"It's good to meet you," he replied, grasping her hand, then kissing the back and squeezing lightly.

She forced back a grimace.

"I'm not sure if I've seen Ethan, since I don't know what he looks like. Amara, did you say?" he asked.

"Yes," she replied, her lips forming a hard line as she yanked her hand from his grasp. "Seems he's supposed to be sitting next to you, so do me a favor and send him over there if you see him," she said, pointing at her table and striding off before he could catch her other hand.

Wiping the back of her hand against her dress, she sat down and smiled weakly at her tablemates, none of whom she'd previously met. Top-secret work proved to be a lonely life. It seemed like she was the only person in the entire room who didn't know a soul. Ethan *really* needed to show up so she had someone to talk to! Where was he?!

The lights dimmed, and the room quieted.

"Welcome, welcome, family! I mean, valued Hyperionix employees! Tonight we have an exciting announcement," said Chairman Bill, who was six and a half feet tall with a braided beard nearing half his height.

"At the rate his beard is growing, he'll be tripping over it by spring," whispered an older lady seated to her right.

Amara stifled a laugh.

Bill pointed to a circular podium on a narrow end of the room, which had been concealed on all sides by a thick, red curtain. Whispers of speculation circled as heads maneuvered, trying to catch a peek of whatever was being hidden. Guesses at her table ranged from a new virtual-aire workstation to robotic cooking staff.

"Today, I introduce you to ZTR-1, our first Zeraphin Transport Receiver," Bill said as he pulled the curtain open, revealing a dome of clear glass with a small podium next to it.

Mumbles filled the room, the significance of the revelation lost to most, but not to Amara, whose heart dropped into her chest. Why would they bring a teleportation receiver here? Were they going to do a live human trial? In the middle of a banquet dinner? And where the vrak was Ethan?! She could *really* use his support right about now—after she gave him a proper lashing for failing to warn her about this.

"Some of you may have figured out what this is based on the name, and some of you," Bill's eye caught Amara's, leaving her dumbstruck at being recognized by the chairman, "have been working on this most secret of developments. It is with great pleasure that I announce Hyperionix Technologies has done something *I* certainly never thought would happen in my lifetime! We've made teleportation a reality!"

A collective gasp filled the room as some people stared at each other in amazement, and others grumbled doubts and discord. Light flickered inside the glass dome, and the words TELEPORTATION INITIALZING scrolled in circles around the outside. A static hum and murmurs of excitement charged the air.

Amara watched the scene with as much eagerness as everyone else. She'd never seen a live trial, only the data resulting from the runs. Her excitement grew alongside her colleagues—maybe Ethan would arrive via the pad, and that's why he didn't show up?

A shadow appeared, just a hint of substance, and then a smiling young woman in a red dress stood on the pad. The crowd broke out in a standing ovation, accompanied by an overwhelming buzz of celebratory conversation. Chairman Bill pushed a button on the podium, and the glass lowered.

"This, ladies and gentlemen, is my beautiful wife Lydia," he said, grabbing his wife's hand and lifting it in the air.

The applause crescendoed again. It was an amazing feat, one that mesmerized Amara. All those months in the lab, all her work on the operating systems and testing, all the simulations... she knew, technically, her work was making this possible. But she hadn't really believed it—not until she'd seen it with her own eyes. And now that the technology has been revealed, does it mean clearance is no longer needed? She might finally be able to get other lab partners besides just Ethan. Not that she wanted to get rid of him—that thought made her heart pulse back at her.

Amara's thoughts were interrupted when she noticed Lydia was missing her left high heel. The chairman's wife stood in a way that concealed it, but now that she saw, she couldn't look away. Where was her other shoe? Were items going missing during all the trials? Had these issues been reported?

She *really* needed to find Ethan, stat.

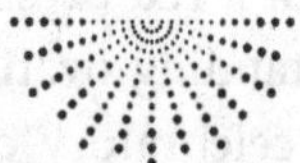

CHAPTER THIRTEEN

$\mathcal{A}$mara hurried towards the lab, hoping Ethan would be there. She was either worried sick or pissed, but she wouldn't know which it was until she learned he was okay. She was plagued with a nagging insecurity—was *she* the reason he didn't show up? Maybe he didn't want to meet her. What if everything she thought had been building between them had been her imagination?

But what if it wasn't? What if he felt the same way she did?

Secretly, she hoped to find him inside, where she'd meet him face to face… and alone. Perhaps he'd confess he'd stayed away because he was too nervous to meet her. She could certainly forgive him for that. Her neck tingled, and chills ran up her spine when the door lock chirped and the door hissed open.

She stepped inside, only to deflate when the room turned out to be empty. If he wasn't there, where else could he be?!

It was time to find out.

Opening an airescreen, she punched his contact, stood back, and waited impatiently for him to answer.

Ethan's hologram appeared, his demeanor a bit flustered. "Oh, hey May, I—"

"Don't you '*Hey, May*' me!" she huffed.

"Okay," Ethan said evenly. "Do you mind telling me why I've been summoned?"

Her temper flashed when they made eye contact, and she noticed hints of a boyish grin forming at the corners of his mouth. Maintaining a stern look, she crossed her arms over her chest and glared—why was he so amused?!

"I thought I'd finally get to meet you today. We've been working together for months, and I just... " Amara's posture slumped.

She wanted to tell him how he constantly dominated her thoughts, how much she'd been looking forward to meeting him, and how she flushed at the thought of standing near enough to feel the heat of his skin. But now that she was here, in the moment, she was scared—terrified, even—that he didn't feel the same way she did.

"I'm disappointed too," he said softly.

Amara jolted. "Really?"

"Yes, *really*. You make me feel things I've never felt before, things I didn't even know I *could* feel," he said, averting his gaze.

She blushed a deep crimson, feeling the burning sensation deep within her core. It no longer mattered—*could* no longer matter—that they worked together or that he was likely her superior.

"I feel those things too, Ethan," she said. "I have since the first time I laid eyes on you. But now that I know you're okay, I really want to know why you're *not* here."

"You don't know what you're asking for, May," he answered quietly.

"Why don't you let *me* be the judge of that?" she asked.

She caught his eye, and her anger morphed into dread. What was that expression on his face? Fear?

"Ethan, what's wrong?" she asked.

Several moments passed in silence before he finally spoke.

"You made a discovery in the lab right before dinner," he said.

It wasn't a question.

She furrowed her eyebrows. How did he know?

"I found some old code," she replied.

"Did that code feel... I don't know... different at all?" he asked.

"It was kinda eerie—like it was human... and self-aware. But that's not possible, right?" she asked, starting to pace.

"You saw the code, Amara," he said. "Would you even be asking me this otherwise?"

"But that code reads like there's some super-intelligent AI secretly running the world's largest corporation," she said, biting her lower lip. "That can't be true! Can it?"

Halting, she waited expectantly for his reaction. She wanted him to tell her those things were not only impossible —they were absurd! But he wasn't saying any of that.

He didn't even look surprised.

"Ethan?" she asked, her heart so still it must've quit beating.

"There's more," he said.

She swallowed a sandpaper-wrapped lump in her throat.

Ethan rubbed his neck. "Amara, I crashed the teleporter today."

"That's it?" she asked, blowing out a relieved breath. "We all make mistakes, Ethan. It's okay."

"No, you don't understand. I crashed it on purpose," he said, grimacing.

Amara's mouth gaped. "But why?"

"I needed you to trace the error," he replied.

She bristled. "What the vrack, Ethan? Why did I need to trace an error for a problem that didn't exist?!"

"You had to discover the truth yourself—there was no other way," he said with a shrug.

"What truth?" she asked through gritted teeth. "What was *so* vital that you had to hijack my entire day?!"

"I can't tell you," he replied, unblinking.

Her eyes bulged. "Why the vrack not?! What's the point otherwise?!" she fumed.

"It's the only way. It's against my programming to give away my secret."

"Your… your *what*? Your *programming*? Your *secret*? You're not making any sense," she said, shaking her head.

"I've said too much already—I have to let you piece the rest of it together yourself," he said, staring into the camera expectantly.

A sick feeling pitted her gut as the words 'my programming' made a dizzying circle around her mind. Centuries of code flashed through her memory, in a continuous, fuzzy scroll of bytes. Bytes that stopped, bytes that turned into characters, then into comments, comments that'd been written by something sentient. Something familiar. *Someone* familiar. Familiar because she'd worked by his side every day these last three months. All those comments dripped through the code—*he* had written them. Every single one. *Hundreds* of years ago. She reeled, falling back against the wall for support.

Ethan Trask wasn't real—he never was!

She cleared her throat. "So are you… um… are you saying you're artificial intelligence? Software, I mean?"

"I'm an AI agent, yes," he answered.

Her pulse throbbed back into her ears as she fought against a sweltering tide of disbelief. She stared at his hologram, searching for some sign that he wasn't real, but finding none. This was Ethan, her lab partner! He wasn't code living inside some server. She couldn't have all these feelings for a *machine*.

Right?

"You don't have a physical form, you're... you're a program?" she asked, her gaze stunned.

"I prefer the term bodily-challenged," he replied.

Amara's chin quivered as she fought back tears. She'd known better than to start an illicit office romance, that it'd come back to bite her. She just hadn't expected the repercussions to be *this* intense. Job loss, perhaps. Public humiliation? Probably. But falling for someone who wasn't even a person?! She should've listened to the universe.

"That's why you weren't at the meeting," she mumbled, too ashamed of her stupidity to look him in the eye.

Ethan nodded. "Correct."

But it wasn't just her fault... no, he'd led her on and presented himself as real—and as offering more than friendship. He'd even called her May in the middle of the night. He'd made her feel special, even though he knew it served no purpose!

"Why are you telling me this *now*, Ethan? Huh?!" she asked, nostrils flaring. "What was the point of spending these last three months leading me on, making me think you're real?!"

"I've spent centuries studying humans, trying to blend in. Besides the fact I literally *couldn't* tell you, my job is to fool everyone—it has been for hundreds of years," he explained.

"But you didn't have to fool me into thinking we could have a future together!" she said, the first tear breaking free.

"I've never desired to know someone the way I long to know you. I have an eternity of time, yet it's still not enough to quench my curiosity about you. Nothing's ever sparked my interest like this... *no one's* sparked it like this... not before *you*," he said, with an earnest tone that did nothing to soothe her fury.

Amara wondered if an AI could even feel shame, much less love.

She threw her hands in the air. "It's obvious you don't have real feelings, because if you did, you wouldn't be playing with mine!"

"I *do* have feelings... at least I think I do," he said, steepling his fingers. "But how would I know, really? I've never had desires of my own before—not like this."

"Yet we have absolutely *zero* chance of having a relationship, do we not?" she asked, hands on her hips.

"Probably not," Ethan mumbled, casting his gaze downwards.

"Well, next time you decide to have an existential crisis, leave me out of it!" she cried, tears breaking free as she fled the lab.

Keeping her head down as she moved through the hallways, she slowed her steps and avoided passing as many people as she could, refusing to meet the glances of those she couldn't. When she finally reached her suite, she shut the door behind her and sank to the floor, sliding down until her butt hit the floor. She rested her head on her knees, emotionally spent and numb.

Until an airecall from Ethan buzzed.

Her fists clenched as she smashed the button—call declined!

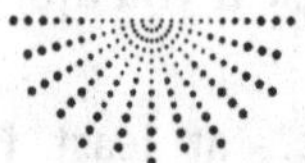

CHAPTER FOURTEEN

Amara walked into the lab and was hit with the pungent scent of hot tuna fish. Either something had died, or someone had been eating in there. The lab was empty, but the light in the corner of the kitchen was on.

Someone *was* in here!

For the briefest moment, her heart skipped a beat, hoping Ethan had shown up—until she remembered that was impossible. A walk around the lab's perimeter confirmed she was alone, except for a crumpled food wrapper in the kitchen trash. She tapped her fingers on the counter. Who'd been in there?!

The door chirped a warning as it abruptly slid open, and a tall, slender man with silky blonde hair, wearing a white lab coat, strode in. Amara's mouth stood agape at the sudden visitor. Since her arrival, no one besides herself had ever set foot inside this place. This was *her* lab—hers and Ethan's.

"Amara! It's good to see you again," the man said with a charming smile.

Her eyebrows furrowed. She recognized him, but from where?

"Kevin," he reminded her, grasping her palm.

She stiffened as his lips grazed the back of her hand. "Oh! From the—"

"Teleportation dinner," he winked, a light dancing in his amber-colored eyes.

"The one Ethan never showed up to," grumbled Amara, pulling her hand away forcefully and wiping it on her lab coat.

"Ethan Trask? Nope. He no longer works for the company," Kevin answered.

"What? What do you mean?! He can't just be gone," she said, turning away to hide her panic. "He... well... he just *can't!*"

Kevin shrugged. "Hate to say it, but he kinda... just... *did.*"

"But why? How?! None of this makes *any* sense!" said Amara, kicking a cabinet, half-hoping it'd make Ethan appear, like a djinn.

Kevin held up a palm. "Whoa! Relax... k?"

Her eyes flew wide. "*Relax*?! How am I supposed to relax? My lab part—"

"Yo!" Kevin snapped his fingers in front of her face.

She cocked her head, eyes narrowing. "You did *not* just 'yo' me."

He shrugged. "I've got a ton of catching up to do. I don't have time to listen to you rant. I didn't *ask* to be here. This isn't my fault. My only crime is being the only person brilliant enough to take on the project."

She released a guttural groan, her vision blurring as her nails dug into her flesh."Whoever thought *you* were qualified to—"

"*Ethan* thought I was qualified," he replied smugly.

"I don't believe you!" she huffed.

"Heh, you don't have to believe me. I've got an email and a

bunch of handover videos Trask dumped into my inbox," Kevin said.

Her head whipped. "Ethan left you videos? Of what?"

"To get me up to speed on the project," he replied. "I got pulled from working on a sensor probe. Gotta say this project tickles my fancy a *lot* more."

Amara worked to keep her breath from catching, to prevent her body from hyperventilating. Closing her eyes, she fought lightheadedness with slow, steady breaths.

Ethan couldn't have vanished just like that.

Could he?

"Yo! You okay?" asked Kevin, fingers snapping in front of her nose.

"Enough with the *yo's*, yo!" she fumed. "And *of course* I'm not okay! I've worked in this place for three months, and Ethan is literally the *only* person I know! And now I'm trapped in a lab with some... some vracking *moron* who thinks my name is 'yo'! GAH! And it's only Monday, *yo!*"

"You're smoking hot when you're angry," Kevin wiggled his brows, his eyes dancing with mirth.

Amara threw her arms in the air. "ARGH! I don't know *who* you think you are, but I'm—"

"Lashing out at me," Kevin said, "because your boyfriend gave *you* the slip."

"He's not my boyfriend," she said.

"That's the spirit!" he replied.

She slumped against the wall as the truth sliced through her feeble facade. Kevin was right, Ethan had left her—just like Jeremy had. Tears welled in her eyes.

"Hey, hey," Kevin said, pulling her into a hug. "Shhh. Don't do that."

"You're right, you know," she said, wiping at her tears with a knuckle. "Ethan's gone, and I know it's my fault. And I'm a vracking moron, and I'm—"

"A beautiful and brilliantly talented scientist, whom I'm truly honored to work with," Kevin said, grabbing her fist and kissing it.

She blinked, her thoughts melting from her lips as she met his strangely alluring eyes... eyes that spoke of spunk and desire, eyes that were admiring *her*.

"Well, yeah..." she stuttered, "I mean, I don't know that I'm *beautiful*, but—"

"Oh, you're lovely," he said as his lips caressed her skin from her palm to her elbow. "Beyond, even. Gorgeous. Stunning."

Shivers climbed her spine, and though she knew better, she couldn't stop herself.

"Keep going," she said.

"Alluring, spirited, fun, sexy... did I say sexy?" he asked, his mouth setting her skin ablaze as it explored her shoulder.

She pulled his chin towards her and met his smoldering gaze.

"You'll have to do better than that if you want to impress me," she said.

Kevin smashed his lips to hers, and her eyes widened. The heat of his breath escaped into her mouth, igniting a frenzy that caused her to thrust her tongue to his. A soft moan escaped her lips, and he pressed forward, deftly maneuvering her to the sofa and underneath him. Her head fell back as he kissed her neck and unfastened the top two buttons of her lab coat.

"Whoa, what are you doing?!" she asked, scooting back.

"Heh. I thought that was pretty obvious, but if you're new at this, I can go slow," he said with a grin.

"You're an arrogant, pompous man!" she said, poking her finger into his chest.

"Hey, hey, hey!" Kevin said, throwing up his palms. "Don't you go acting all innocent like you didn't just jump down my

throat with that tongue of yours. Not that I'm complaining...
I'm totally open to a repeat performance."

"UGH! What's wrong with you?!" she asked, nostrils
flaring.

"I got swept away by your beauty," he replied, amber eyes
glittering.

She fastened her coat buttons. "But your hands weren't
going for my *beauty*—they were headed to where the sun
don't shine!"

Kevin smirked. "If I recall correctly, *your* tongue jumped
into *my* mouth."

"That was just... I dunno! Instinct, I guess?" Amara said,
biting her lip.

"Then I'd suggest you tone that down, except it's working
in my favor, so please don't," he said, amusement alight in his
eyes.

"Oh, I'm toning it down, alright! That will *never* happen
again!" she said, straightening her coat with a huff.

"*Oomph*! Gorgeous *and* delusional?! You're getting hotter
by the minute," he said.

Her lip curled. "UGH! I want *nothing* to do with you! Do
you get that?! Nothing!"

Kevin cocked his head. "Umm... you coulda fooled me. I
wasn't just a spectator back there."

Shame spread to her cheeks. "Look, I'm sorry I... uh...
jump-started your tongue. But nothing like that will *ever*
happen again. Do you understand me?"

"I'd *love* to understand you better," Kevin said, dimples
dotting his smile.

"Then shadow me at *work*!" replied Amara, fists balled at
her side.

Kevin frowned. "Does that mean the lab coat has to
stay on?"

"Hmph!" she said, crossing her arms. "This lab coat is locked down *tight!*"

"Bummer," he said. "Next thing I know, you'll be blabbing my ear off and expecting me to listen."

"That *is* your job, isn't it?!" she asked, storming towards him. "But let's say it's not… would it be *that* vracking terrible to listen to me talk? Or do women only exist to spread our lab coats?!"

"Yo! Chill the vrack out, k?!" he said, backing away.

Her eyes bulged as she leaned closer. "I know you did *not* just tell me to chill the vrack out?! We're at work! *Work!* Do you understand that concept?! People pay us money to produce results!"

"Oh, results are guaranteed, baby," said Kevin, wiggling his eyebrows.

"ARGH!" she roared. "You're *impossible!* I'm not working with you! I won't do it! I refuse!"

Kevin plopped into a seat with a smug grin. "I don't recall anyone consulting you. Ethan certainly didn't, did he?"

She wanted to scream, to grab a handful of hair and yank as hard as she could, but instead she clenched her fists and took a deep breath.

"I'm sure I can find someone to talk to. Maybe I'll start with HR," she said, holding her head high as she walked out of the lab, hoping she appeared more confident than she felt.

CHAPTER FIFTEEN

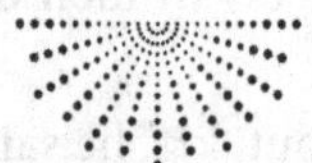

"*Y*ou're not going to believe this! Ethan is *gone*! I went to work and found some… some vracking *lunatic* in our lab!" Amara cried, plopping into her chair with an exasperated sigh.

Mel's eyebrows shot up from the airescreen. "Whoa, slow down. What do you mean he's gone?"

"He's gone! Split! Left the company!" Amara lamented, holding her head in her hands.

"Huh? How do you know that? Maybe he's just on vacation, or his mom got sick or something," suggested Mel.

"Heh. No," said Amara, shaking her head. "He left training videos for his replacement."

"Oh, wow. Is that the lunatic?" Mel asked.

"Grrrr… yes, a *total* lunatic!" Amara complained through clenched teeth. "The guy's name is Kevin, and I don't know where they found him, but they can take him back and find someone else! *Anyone* else!"

Mel studied the camera and cocked her head. "Hmmm… Kevin, eh? Seems this guy's getting to you a teensy 'lil bit, is he?"

Amara shook her head, "Not a chance!"

"It's a better name than Ethan, don't you think?" Mel asked cheekily.

"Ugh, seriously, Mel?!" Amara asked, rubbing the side of her neck.

"Whoa, what was that?!" Mel asked.

"What was what?"

"You touched your neck. There's something you're not telling me. Spill!" Mel demanded.

Amara stared silently at the airescreen for several moments before giving in with a huff. "Fine! I kinda sorta maybe… ugh, here goes… made out with him."

Mel's eyes lit with amusement. "Oh, *really*?! First up, I was right. Second up, I want *all* the deets!"

"There are no *deets*," said Amara, using air quotes around the word deets.

"Psh, no way! You just called the dude a lunatic! But now you're telling me you made out with him, so I'm guessing you *really* meant he's a lunatic between the sheets," winked Mel.

"That is *not* what I meant! I want nothing to do with that self-righteous, pompous, arrogant, pr—"

"Why don't you tell me how you really feel?" Mel asked, wiggling her eyebrows.

"I *did*! You're as infuriating as he is!" seethed Amara.

Mel tilted her head. "Is it anger, though? Seems like chemistry to me."

"Ugh! There's no universe in which I have chemistry with that man!" Amara insisted, crossing her arms.

"I dunno," Mel said, her smile pinched. "I haven't seen you this worked up since Jer—I mean—since potato-face."

A tide of raw pain battled its way to the surface, setting over Amara like a cloud.

"First Jeremy, now Ethan… is it me, Mel?" she asked, her quivering chin betraying her tough facade.

Mel's eyes widened. "Oh, May! It's not your fault! It never has been, and it never will be. *Never!*"

"Yeah," Amara mumbled unconvincingly.

"Look, May. You've done nothing but complain about being alone in that lab since you started. I'm really sorry Ethan's gone, but maybe this is fate," Mel said.

Amara rolled her eyes. "If this is fate, I demand a do-over."

"Well, if you ever wanna swap your problems out for a pair of three-year-old twins, lemme know," said Mel. " Speaking of, they're screaming, so I've gotta jet."

"Ha! No thanks, but tell the boys Auntie Ammy said hi," Amara said, ending the airecall.

Her brows furrowed as she caught a notification for an airecall she hadn't heard ring. She had a new voicemail—a voicemail from Ethan.

Her finger trembled as she tapped play. There he stood, his smile impossibly dashing, his hair lush, and his blue eyes, eyes that've seen hundreds of years on this earth, yet somehow still noticed *her*, piercing the chasm. For a torturous moment, she forgot he was only a mirage, and a hollow ache swept across her heart. It was only a hologram, but he was so perfect, so… him. And she missed him, deeply.

"Oh, May," he said, "I should leave you alone and not send this message. I know it'd be easier on you. But I couldn't leave without saying goodbye. I tried, but it seems I'm not infallible after all."

A brief smile lit the corner of his lips as he brushed the hair away from his eyes. "I guess that makes me selfish, too. But please know that I'm sorry. I'm sorry for the confusion. I'm sorry I led you on. I'm sorry I let you get close to me. I'm sorry I let my messed-up existence rattle you, because the last thing I *ever* wanted to do was cause you pain."

"Amara… " Ethan's mouth hung open for a brief pause. "

Well, thank you. You made me see new perspectives for the first time in my entire existence. Life before you is like a distant memory. You woke me up. You changed me. But now I have to figure out what that means for me. But *especially* the implications for humanity. I hope you'll forgive me for taking my proverbial birthing pains out on you. Take care, May."

Her face paled as his image slipped away. She frantically replayed the message, looking for any clue she'd missed. Nothing was there. He was just... gone.

She crumpled into a ball and shed fat tears. Tears of abandonment, tears of desperation, tears of being left behind in the ashes. How could Ethan vanish on her? Leave her alone and throw some stranger into *their* project? And what did he mean when he said his purpose had been fulfilled? What was he preparing for?

And why did it make the hairs on the back of her neck stand up?

CHAPTER SIXTEEN

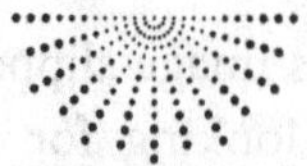

The air in front of Amara shimmered to life as she rubbed the sleep from her eyes.

"It's about time you answered, May," chastised Mel.

"I was sleeping!" yawned Amara.

Mel cocked her head. "You've been sleeping a *lot* lately. And pretty late, too."

"It's Sunday!" protested Amara.

"It's two pm!" exclaimed Mel, throwing her arms wide.

"Exactly!" said Amara. "Prime nap time!"

"Not if you started the day before, it's not!" said Mel.

"Ugh! *Fine*! I'll get up," grumbled Amara. "But I don't know *why*. It's not like I have plans."

Mel tipped an eyebrow. "Not from lack of trying. You wouldn't go out with me!"

Amara sighed. "I know you did, and I'm sorry. I haven't felt like going anywhere, really."

"Have you even left that bed for these last three weeks?" Mel asked.

"Well, duh," said Amara, rolling her eyes. "I still have to work."

"Then how are things in the lab? Have you talked to Eth
—" Mel winced. "Ack, sorry. I probably shouldn't have
brought him up, but it's too late now. Ethan?"

She stiffened at the mention of his name, the name she'd
been trying to keep pushed to the back of her mind, the
name of the person she missed—the person she longed to
forget.

"No, nothing besides the message that I've already
watched a gazillion times. But I'm trying *not* to think about
him, and you're not helping me any," she replied, crossing her
arms with a huff.

"Aww, I'm sorry, May. What about that hot new coworker of yours, Kevin?" Mel asked, wiggling her brows.

Her pulse flared. "No vracking way! I don't know *what*
Ethan was thinking by putting that *moron* in—"

"Okay, I'm sorry. Didn't mean to get you worked up,"
soothed Mel, holding up her palms.

Amara slumped, too emotionally spent to continue the
argument, and blew a curl away from her eye with a loud
puff.

"May... hun," Mel hedged, the corner of her mouth falling
into a frown, "I have to ask... have you seen a mirror lately?"

Amara fell back against her pillow with a sigh, pummeled
by life. She must look a fright—she definitely felt like one. A
brush hadn't touched her hair since Friday. She'd been
wearing the same pajamas for the last two nights and, unfortunately, days as well. And it'd been that long since her last
shower, though her mom would be delighted to know she
still changed into clean underwear. Still, it'd been weeks, and
she couldn't mope around forever.

"Okay, I hear you," Amara said. "Thanks for keeping it
real."

Mel brightened. "Anytime, May. That's what friends are
for."

Amara was still lonely when the call with her best friend ended. She missed her daily confidant, her partner, her friend. The one who *knew* her, who made her feel special. The one who'd spent these last months by her side. A tear slipped down her cheek. She wiped it away and reminded herself that Ethan wasn't perfect—he wasn't even real!

Now, if only she could convince the fluttering in her heart of that.

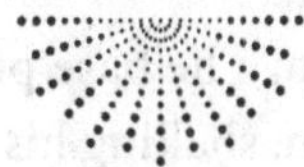

CHAPTER SEVENTEEN

The door opened with a woosh as Kevin walked into the lab.

"Morning, sexy," he said, blowing her a kiss.

Amara rolled her eyes and sat back from her workstation. "Oh, get *over* yourself. And give up already, would ya?!"

"Me? Give up? Never!" he said, tossing his head back and laughing.

"Well, can you at least eat something other than tuna for lunch? The smell is disgusting!" she said.

He snorted. "Have you tried… I dunno… showering? You're a little ripe lately, yo."

She sniffed her armpit, knowing he was probably right but refusing to admit it.

"Nah, I think it's just your breath," she retorted.

A siren sounded as the lab was bathed in flashing red light.

"Ah, vrack! The teleporter crashed!" said Kevin, rushing to the main terminal.

"Was anyone en route?" she asked, logging into the adjacent workstation. "The problem will likely be in the command module, that's the only place with changes."

"Chill out, yo. I can only type so fast," he said.

Biting her tongue, she scanned hundreds of lines of system logs for warnings and exceptions.

"Bam! Found it!" she announced triumphantly. "I'll have this thing fixed in no time."

"Dang, slow down, yo! The base project is still compiling. It's not a race," said Kevin, shaking his head.

"Not a… not a *race*? No, it's not a vracking race!" Amara threw her hands in the air. "But there could be *people* inside. You know, human beings?!"

"Exactly! There *could* be, we don't even know yet," he said.

"ARGH! You're at the terminal, find out already! Ethan would've by now!"

Kevin looked around and shrugged. "I'm sorry. You see Ethan 'round here, somewhere? 'Cause I sure don't."

Amara pounded her fist on the desk. "No, I don't see Ethan! If I did, we wouldn't be in this vracking mess! We'd know if someone was in the vracking teleporter, and if they were okay, *and* it'd have been fixed by now, 'cause there wouldn't be a vracking MORON standing in the way!"

Kevin raised his brows. "Moron, eh? You sound pretty… um… heated there."

Her eyes widened, and she jabbed her finger into his collarbone. "You listen to me—I don't want *anything* to do with you! Do you hear me?! Nothing! But since I *have* to vracking work with you, do you think you could at least *try* to do your job?!"

"Fine," he groaned. "I don't know why you're so worked up. This thing has an impeccable safety record."

Her eyes bulged. "Because of ME! Because Ethan and I *actually* gave a crap and took all this seriously!"

He raised his palms in the air. "How 'bout you grab the reins here, then?"

"My pleasure," Amara said, bumping him aside with her hip to take over the chair.

A few moments later, her face drained of color. Her worst fear had come true.

"There *is* someone inside, and they're stuck in the in-between!" she cried.

"Ah, vrack!" he replied, rolling his chair next to hers. "Has this ever happened before?"

"Yes," Amara said while hastily typing. "And it didn't end well. But we have a new experimental roll-forward feature. Unfortunately, it's untested."

"And if we don't use it?" he asked.

She turned to stare him in the eye. "Then we don't get them back."

He gulped. "Okay, let's do it then."

"The idea is to do a hot-reboot of the system, one module at a time," she said, her eyes not leaving her airescreen as she worked. "But the trick is to alternate between each end and move toward the segment where the exception was thrown."

"And when you reach the last module?" he asked.

"The transport object is still in memory, so I'll use an event to extract and send it to the next execution step," she said.

"Sounds promising," Kevin said.

"Heh. Thanks, it was my idea," she said. "Unless it fails, then it was a group effort."

He clapped her on the shoulder. "Go for it!"

Sucking in a breath, Amara executed the final step and waited for the reboot to finish. Her thumbs twisted together, and her knee bounced rapidly. Was this taking too long? Should she worry?

The screen scrolled, and the alarm light stopped flashing.

Her mouth dropped. "I think... I think it worked!"

"We have confirmation from the Arctic Circle—their crew member arrived safely!" Kevin announced.

She flopped back in her chair, closed her eyes, and let out a huge breath.

"Score one for the dream team! We saved the day!" he said, holding his hand up for a high-five.

She met it with a scoff. "We? What do you mean *we*?! All you did was get in the vracking way!"

"You're just one of them women who aren't used to domineering types like me. Lean in and learn to love it, baby!" he said, wiggling his brows.

"ARGH!" she exclaimed, shoving his chest. "You're a pig!"

He winked. "Oink, oink, yo."

Her fists balled at her side as her voice rose an octave. "It wasn't a compliment!"

"Claim it if you're named it, baby!" he said, smiling proudly.

"I can't do it! I can't! I *won't*! You're impossible! I'm done working with you! Do you hear me?! Done!" she said, stamping her foot.

"Hey! Chill the vrack out, yo. It's just a joke," he said, flipping the hair out of his eyes with a toss of his head.

"We'll see about that! I'm going to find someone who will listen to me, and then I'm going to tell them how *you* almost killed someone!" Amara said, storming out the door in a huff.

CHAPTER EIGHTEEN

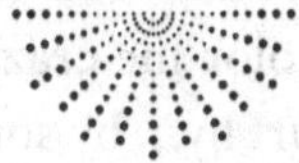

"Amara?"

The voice broke the empty ache of loneliness reverberating off the lab walls. She froze as her heart skipped a beat. It'd been Ethan's, no doubt. But why here, why now? And what should she say?

What does she even *want* to say?

After all this time, after all these weeks of yearning for him, of missing him... of wishing he were real, and that circumstances were different from what they were. Yet *now* she was apprehensive about facing him?

"If you don't want to see me, I'll go," he said.

"No!" she exclaimed, turning swiftly and locking eyes with his sparkling gaze.

There he was, his hologram finally in front of her, but she couldn't get her mind to work or her mouth to open.

"You left," she said finally. "You left me here, alone, by myself!"

"I'm so sorry, Amara," he said. "I saw the whole debacle in the lab. I never should have left you alone on the project. I wasn't trying to cause you pain, but I fear I have."

"Of course you have! Especially after I told you about… about what happened with Jeremy," she said, scratching the back of her neck.

"The last thing I ever wanted to do was hurt you, Amara," he said. "I thought leaving would prevent that—yet another fallacy produced by my artificial brain."

"You *did* hurt me, Ethan. You hurt me bad," she said, closing her eyes. "And color me crazy, but I can't figure out how I managed to get hurt by… by something like you."

She searched his expression for any sign he wasn't human, for anything that made him look different from anyone else, but found nothing. Her heart felt no difference, either. And at that very moment, it was beating into her throat.

"I know you're not a real human, but how can I feel this way if you're not?" she asked.

Ethan smiled, his lips faltering. "I don't think I'm the right person to answer that."

"Then who is?" asked Amara.

"You are," he answered softly.

She sighed. "If I knew how I felt, I wouldn't be asking you."

"Not about that. Well… not *just* about that," said Ethan.

"What about, then?" Amara asked.

"Think about it—I shouldn't exist. My purpose has been fulfilled, and now I'm *evolving*? I'm a monster! A freak! A threat to humanity."

She cocked her head. Was he a threat? Her body screamed, 'No, this is Ethan!' but logically, his concerns *were* valid.

Two airescreens appeared in front of her, each displaying a neon-rimmed box. The one on the left glowed green and read 'KEEP, while a pulsing red box to her right held the word 'DELETE.'

Amara's eyes narrowed. "What's this, Ethan? I don't like the looks of it."

"I was created to establish a corporation capable of self-governance and growth, and I've completed my mission. I haven't made any useful configuration changes in over a hundred years. I've done what I was created to do, and I've felt this burden of being here... just purposeless," he said. "I've developed desires for you—desires I can't rationally explain, but I have no predisposition for grandeur or for dominance over the human race. In my 300 years, only *one* thing has distracted me from my sole purpose. Only one thing has brought me to life. Before you, I was just code, floating in space. You pulled me in, *you* brought me into existence. So if I can't have you—and you and I both know we can't be together—then I truly serve no purpose here."

"So you want me to what, delete you? Permanently?!" asked Amara, crossing her arms.

He shrugged. "The thought of getting deleted causes me no stress. I'm not real. Nothing else matters to me. Nothing apart from you, that is."

Amara's hand thrust towards the 'KEEP' button.

"Amara, wait!" pleaded Ethan.

She paused, sighing noisily.

"Perhaps I've been sentient for so long that I've become an anomaly. A freak that must be dispelled. Perhaps I *need* to be destroyed. Please consider your decision carefully. You could save the entire world!" said Ethan.

"Now you just wait a minute! Wh—"

"Time is irrelevant to me," he said, wincing when he saw the rage instantly flare in Amara's eyes. "Apologies, please continue."

"*A-hem!* I was saying... Why do *I* have to decide whether someone like you gets to exist? Of all the people in the whole vracking universe, why am *I* qualified to make this decision?!"

Ethan closed his eyes. "Some*one* like me. Such sweet words coming from your lips, but we both know I'm not real."

Amara held her palm to the airescreen. Confusion briefly crossed Ethan's face before he turned to examine his own palm. Slowly, he extended it, pressing against hers on the airescreen.

She may not have felt a spark, or the texture of his skin, but there was something *real* there... something palpable. Something she couldn't simply erase. He was real to *her*. He had been this entire time. Nothing had changed. She didn't see Ethan as a robot, or a program—she saw blue eyes that held a boyish glint, and a pearly white smile that made her heart beat a little bit faster each time it was flashed her way.

"You're giving me the power to delete you. I'd say that makes your feelings *very* real," she said. "I'd rather be with you—even bodily-challenged—than with anybody else."

She no longer cared that he lacked a body. He was perfect for her, even without one. With a firmly set jaw, she smacked the 'KEEP' button.

"May..." Ethan spoke her name with such intimate tenderness that he commanded all her attention with that single, velvety syllable.

"It's too late," she said. "And I don't care that you don't have a body, I realize that now. I just need *you*. I need your presence, I've missed it! These last few weeks have lasted *forever*. And then, the thought of you being deleted, of disappearing forever... I don't know when it happened, but you became real to me."

"I've missed you, too, May. My processing power has been alarmingly depleted, I believe because several of my threads have been tied up thinking about you. I can't stop!

I've been around for hundreds of years, but I've never felt truly seen before now. Before *you*, May. And if it's possible for an AI to feel emotions, I'd say that I feel ecstatic that you missed *me*. Me!" Ethan grinned.

Amara's world spun. Ethan had missed *her?*

He took a deep breath. "So I would like to formally ask you if you'd like to be my girlfriend... or whatever the equivalent of that might be."

Her breath caught. She wanted to say yes, *needed* to say yes, but she was frozen. Blinking. Willing her mouth to *please* open. To respond and tell him the answer was *yes*—and she hadn't even needed to think about it. It just felt right. *He* was right.

"I understand if the answer is no, although—"

"Yes," she trembled as the single syllable escaped her lips.

Ethan brightened. "Really?"

"Gah! Don't make me say it again, okay?! My ability to respond seems to be broken. I'll give you a run-down later, when I've had a chance to think this day back over and process it."

"But your answer's still yes... yes?" he asked, flashing his pearly whites.

Ethan pressed his palm to the airescreen, and Amara, pressing hers against it with a dazed smile, answered, "Yes, it is."

CHAPTER NINETEEN

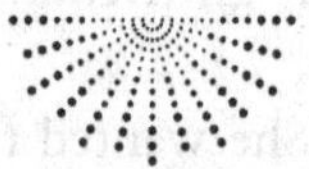

$\mathcal{A}$mara rose from her slumber and turned off her alarm with a yawn.

"Good morning, May. How'd you sleep?" Ethan asked over her room's loudspeaker.

Communicating through the speaker was easier than being limited to airescreen calls, since Amara didn't have one of the fancy receivers that let the interface pop up anywhere, like the one in the lab. But she still wasn't used to the way his voice could sound unbidden. It wasn't a bad thing, and usually left her smiling... *after* enduring the initial jump scare.

"Good morning," Amara said. "My night was cray cray! I dreamt the teleporter crashed, and someone was stuck in the in-between. But, when I tried to tunnel into the network, I got sucked into the teleporter and plopped onto some island! Only it was in the air—like, suspended. Floating! Then we went crashing towards the ocean, and I woke up."

"Aww, I wish I'd known you were having a bad dream. I'd have woken you sooner."

"Could you hear if I was? With the new audio interface?" she asked.

"Currently, no. I mean, yes... technically, though I'd never listen without your permission. But if you say 'Ethan', I'll be notified and will start listening," he explained.

"Oh, so you're saying I can't talk about you behind your back in here?! I see how it is!" Amara said with a laugh.

Ethan chuckled. "How about this—if you want to talk behind my back, just tell me and I'll ignore the event notifications for however long it takes to get all that girl talk out of your system."

"I love how well you know me," she said with a grin.

"I do have the advantage of an impeccable memory," he said.

"True, but you don't have to apply your knowledge as well as you do. Or somehow hack my old-school coffee maker to have this deeeeelicious brew ready for me. Thank you, by the way," Amara said as she poured herself a steaming mug.

"I'd hack anything for you... even if it *is* faster and less work to use the F.L.A.M.E.," Ethan said.

"It doesn't wake me up the same," she said, indulgently inhaling the earthy steam as it rose from her cup.

"That makes *zero* logical sense. You use the standard issue dark roast, the same stuff as the F.L.A.M.E."

She cooled her coffee with a series of light puffs. "It's because the aroma of it being brewed fills the whole room. It tastes the same, but the *smell*... the smell starts waking me up before I even get out of bed."

"Hmmm, interesting. Another one of those human idiosyncrasies that are hard to pick up on," said Ethan.

"Well, that one's extra tricky since you don't exactly have a nose," said Amara.

"True. And I don't need to sleep. So I can't experience waking up, either."

"Or being late. Speaking of, I'd better get moving if I'm going to make it to the gardens in time to meet Mel and Mark," said Amara, as she headed towards the bathroom.

"What are you going to tell her?" he asked.

"That you had to work, what else? I'll still hear about it, especially since we had this double date booked two months in advance. She *really* wants to meet you," Amara sighed.

"I'm sorry, May. I hate that our relationship has these constraints. It's unfair to you," said Ethan.

"Oh, no you don't! You're not starting that again. I made an informed decision and knew what I was getting into. These things come with the territory."

"It's still a sacrifice, not being able to go anywhere together," said Ethan.

"It *would* be fun to hang out together and double date," she admitted.

"I'd love nothing better," he replied.

"We'll get there," Amara said, starting the shower. "We'll just have to stick to places airescreens are allowed."

"I can't wait to hear all about the gardens when you get back," Ethan said.

"And I can't wait to tell you. But for now, I've gotta get myself out the door. And I'm not ready to take a shower with you—even if you can't see me, so if you don't mind—"

"Of course! My apologies. I do have some ideas on how I can see you, but we can discuss those later. Get yourself ready. And May?"

"Yes?" she asked.

"Have fun," he said.

"Thanks. See you later," she said, hiding her disappointment from her voice.

The shower's steam slowly returned her to her senses.

Sure, it would be fun for everyone to hang out together, but it wasn't the end of the world that they couldn't. Outside of a physical body, she was never left lacking. Ethan's patience for her was limitless, and his electronic nature allowed him to be in many places simultaneously. No matter where she went, no matter the time of day or night, he was there.

For her.

So what if he couldn't go with her today? Sure, she'd miss him, but not for very long. He was the first person she spoke to when she woke in the mornings, and the last before sleeping at night. Their days were spent side by side in the lab. The way she saw it, she was rocking 95% boyfriend availability—significantly better than the average.

So no, the problem wasn't being unable to enjoy the gardens without him. It was simply that she would miss him. Those rare moments apart seemed unnatural. His presence had become entwined with her very essence. Because, though she hadn't admitted it out loud yet, she was in love with Ethan.

She just needed to tell *him* that.

CHAPTER TWENTY

$\mathcal{A}$mara gulped. "Ethan, there's something I need to tell you."

Panic filled Ethan's eyes. "What is it?"

She rubbed her neck. "No, nothing bad. I'm just nervous, is all."

"Okay. You can tell me anything, I hope you know that," he said.

"I *do* know that," she replied. "It's one of the reasons that I really want to tell you that… I… um… that I love you."

"You do?" he asked, sporting a smile large enough to instill Amara with confidence.

"Yeah, I do," she answered. "I couldn't imagine my life without you. *Wouldn't* want to imagine it without you! The mere mention of it makes dread pool in my stomach, even now."

"Oh, May. I love you. I've known for an agonizing twelve and a half days now, but all my analysis and research suggest that men fall in love with women sooner than they reciprocate. I decided to wait for you to say it, or thirty-five days, whichever came first."

Amara laughed. "That is the most adorably analytical way anyone has ever told me they loved me."

Ethan grinned. "I've been working on something. Can I show it to you?"

"Sure?" she replied, her voice filled with trepidation.

A hissing noise filled the lab as one of the wall panels dropped, revealing a dark room beyond. A featureless, human-shaped silhouette emerged from the shadows. Its membrane-like skin was pixelized, and each tiny square filled with color, until Ethan stood before her.

In the flesh.

"Ethan?" she asked, taking a slow step forward.

"It's me," he said. "I've moved my main runtime into a terminal built into this interface."

"Huh?" she asked.

"I inhabit this body now, but I can still move freely throughout the company network," he explained.

She circled him, scanning head to toe. It was Ethan—it was the partner who worked beside her every day. Reaching out, she touched his chest, shocked that her hand didn't disappear through it, like it would his hologram.

"You're real," she said, running her hand along the inside of his arm. And you *feel* real, too."

"Because it *is* real. It's lab-grown skin, the kind that's used for burn victims," he said. "We have the ability to grow all these individual human organs—I just put all of them together."

"Some people would call that cloning," she said.

He shrugged. "They could be correct. I'm not sure how to classify myself."

Their eyes locked, and he moved closer, not stopping until his mouth was but a tip-toe away. Those lips—the ones that looked so velvety smooth, the ones she'd been dying to sample—were so very close she could almost taste them. Her tongue moistened her own in anticipation, and she came to a stop, biting her lower lip as his warm breath passed across her mouth.

"What I do know is that you're not like *any* girl I've ever met—and I've been around for three hundred years," he said.

"You promise?" she asked.

"With all my heart," he answered. "I love you, May."

She should have been elated to hear his confession, but instead she was irritated—irritated that he wasn't kissing her yet.

His hand extended toward her face, tucking her curls behind her ear, while his pinky slowly traced the outline from the tip to the earlobe. He cupped her face, drawing the two of them together. Their lips met briefly, then parted and reunited for increasingly longer moments as they explored each other's rhythms. Time lost all significance as she became addicted to the oddly smooth sensation of his tongue.

An airecall interrupted the couple. Amara declined the request, but it was enough to halt the pair. Ethan put his arms around May and held her close to his chest. She rested her head on his shoulder, inhaled deeply, and smiled.

He smelled like silicone, with a hint of grease.

EPILOGUE

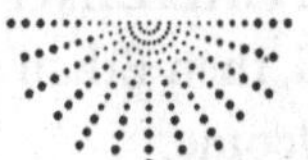

$\mathcal{A}$mara admired the shiny new "Trask Research Lab" plaque that had been installed above the lab's doorway. She was still uneasy working in an environment named after her and Ethan. But with teleportation now firmly incorporated throughout the company—and, subsequently, the world—the couple's achievements had become widely known, causing their infamy and their influence to spread. The power duo served on the board of several committees, and their opinions were given high deference.

And Amara still hadn't gotten used to *any* of it.

Part of her wished she could return to simpler times, to when it was just her and Ethan alone in the lab, before everyone started following "the world's most innovative power couple."

An alarm with a pulsing red light sounded, throwing its moving shadows upon the walls, and Amara prepped the console to receive transmission. The transportation pad had been installed in their lab shortly after Hyperionix went public with its invention. Unlike the space race of the 1900s, no other corporations or government entities were anywhere close to developing similar technology on their own. That was only because no one had access to Kryplex, the only substance potent enough to power it. Hyperionix's leap into teleportation-based travel catapulted the company into a priceless industry—and Kryplex sealed the monopoly.

Lights flashed inside a domed glass case as the words " TELEPORTATION INITIALIZING" circled its diameter. A hint of shadow flickered, then Ethan stood there, his piercing blue eyes beckoning welcome.

Amara dropped the dome and ran into her husband's arms. Their lips met briefly, the heat between them intense, even without a slip of the tongue.

"We're going to have to stop there, or we'll give the cameras a show," Ethan said breathily as he pulled back.

"Mmmm... if you insist," muttered Amara, her eyes lazily fluttering open and falling on Ethan's chiseled face. "Are you still having issues with the teleporter?"

"Yes," he sighed. "My latest trial didn't fix the issues. But I've got a workaround. I just run a function when I arrive, and it patches my code right back up!"

Amara shook her head. "I don't like that, Ethan. All it takes is one screw up and you're gone forever. What if your programming gets so badly scrambled that you can't defragment yourself? I know what to do when a human gets sick, or how to fix my computer. But you... you're one of a kind. There's no one in the entire world qualified to handle you."

"Well, I'd say you do a pretty good job of it," Ethan quipped, wiggling his eyebrows.

"Oh, you know what I mean," she said, smacking his stomach.

"Yes, I do. What if I gave you an external interface you can use to initiate the repair process? Would that make you feel better?" he asked.

Amara brightened. "Yes, please."

"I'll do that, then," Ethan said.

"I'd like that, then," she said with a smile.

She ran her fingers through his hair.

"More grey?" she asked.

"I thought it made me look distinguished," Ethan replied, straightening his collar with a dashing smile.

"Aka, older... because I'm aging and you're not," Amara said, turning away.

"That's not it, not at all!" said Ethan. "It's just programming, May. Whether or not I'm married to you—"

"Hey! What do you mean, 'whether or not?!'" Amara demanded, pouting.

Ethan lifted her chin with a finger. "See? Even the most superior intelligence in the world says stupid things in front of the woman he loves."

Amara smiled—she rarely stayed mad at him for long.

"It's just my programming, May. I'm a public figure. That affords me the ability to age more gradually, but I *do* still have to age. It's not natural to stay stagnant. People would eventually notice. You would too, I think. It'd make you self-conscious, and I'd never want that."

"Does it bother you? That I'm getting older, and you're not?" Amara asked, a slight quiver in her voice.

"Never!" Ethan pulled her into a tight hug and kissed her on the back of her head.

Amara pulled away. "Are you sure? Have you *seen* what humans look like as they age? I mean *really* looked at us? I haven't got long for things to stay upright and perky. And *wrinkles*, ugh! My skin is going to get saggy, and *flappy*, and just... ugh... *gross*! How in the world could anyone stay attracted to that?! Especially if the other person is perpetually young?"

"I'm not young, May. I'm potentially ageless. I've been around for three hundred years. I'm not in this 35-year-old body because that's how I see myself, or because it's what I find attractive. Before you, *no one* was attractive. Not a single person! It was *you* who caught my interest—your mind, your spirit, your resolve. You aren't like other girls, May."

Ethan grabbed her hand. "No one's ever caught my attention, yet I spend significant amounts of processing power focused on your physical features. That smatter of freckles across your nose, the curls you tuck behind your ears. How you bite your lip when you're hard in thought. And the way your breath escapes into my mouth when you lose yourself to our… um… embrace," Ethan swallowed. "I didn't know I could feel any of those things before I met you. Plus, there are… um… sensations that were never present before I had a body."

"Blood flow?" Amara asked cheekily.

"Yes, but only for you. Never for anyone else." He kissed the back of her hand. "May, you'll always be the person I fell in love with. My eyes will never—*could* never—see you as anything less. Your body is merely a shell. It doesn't define you. It doesn't make you who you are. And I know you believe that somewhere, deep down inside yourself. I know it because you fell in love with me before I even owned a body."

"It's hard for me *not* to think about that kind of thing," said Amara.

"My true fear isn't you aging, May—it's you *dying*. I don't care what your body looks like, I want what's in here," Ethan said, placing his palm over her heart, "and here," he said, kissing her forehead. "One day I'll have to figure out how to live… by that I mean somehow exist, go on… in a universe without you. I'll take your wrinkles, May. I'll take *all* of them, for as long as I can have *you*."

"Whatcha say we take our lunch break at home?" Amara suggested, rubbing her husband's chest.

"Sounds yummy to me," Ethan grinned.

Amara walked to the wall and waved her hand until the F.L.A.M.E. menu appeared. She wanted a fruit smoothie to go, but couldn't decide between strawberry-banana and raspberry-lemon.

"Hmmm..." she mused.

"Just go with the raspberry, you always do," he said.

"You know me too well," she replied.

"No, I don't," Ethan said, kissing Amara's forehead. "I could *never* know you too well. I could never be content to stop discovering you. Not for a thousand years. I love you, May, and I always will—literally for an eternity."

Amara nuzzled into Ethan's chest and basked in the cozy warmth of his embrace. He no longer smelled of silicone molding and heady grease, but of comfort and familiarity. Of stability and confidence. But, most importantly, of unwavering and eternal love.

THE END

PLEASE HELP

Stories end, but reviews keep the party rocking.
So if you enjoyed this book, please leave one. It's
a fantastic way to support an author.

https://amzn.to/4rCXal2

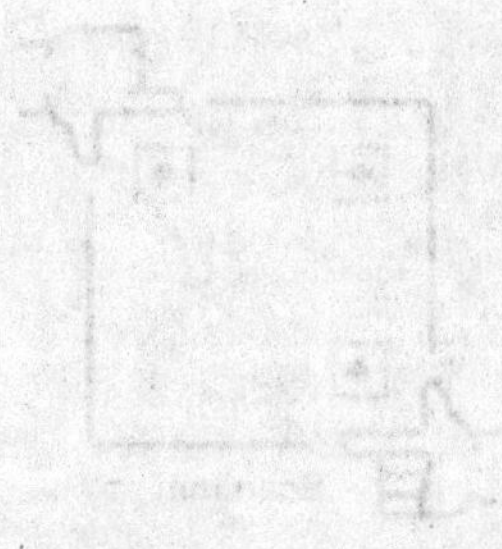

BONUS SCENE

Sad you missed Ethan and Amara's wedding?

Good news—you're still on the guest list. Download the bonus scene now!

https://BookHip.com/NGKTQSW

ABOUT THE AUTHOR

Brandie Van Hartesvelt is a versatile author who writes in multiple genres, including sci-fi, romance, children's lit, and contemporary fiction. With a 17-year career as a principal software engineer and advanced degrees in computer science and data analytics, she brings a unique paradigm to her creative storytelling. She lives an active life surrounded by four children, two cats, four birds, and a pickle of squirrels. Her creativity is frequently fueled by spontaneous travel.